Eavesdropping

Eavesdropping

The River Writers

Eavesdropping

First published 2012 by
The River Writers
660 Berrico Creek Road, Berrico NSW 2422
theriverwriters@gmail.com
Copyright © *The River Writers* 2012

National Library of Australia
Cataloguing-in-Publication entry

The River Writers.

Eavesdropping / The River Writers.

9780987263704   (pbk.)

Short stories.

808.83

Cover design and illustration by
Madeleine Kelman Snow
Photographs by Chris Russell

Printed by Lu Lu Enterprises Inc.
www.lulu.com

Contents

Foreword

Foreword

We're delighted to invite you to eavesdrop on the stories, vignettes and poems we've compiled over our time as the Gloucester U3A Writing Group. The pieces are as interesting and varied as their creators. Some will move you to tears, some you will identify with and we hope many will make you smile.

This anthology has been a genuinely collaborative effort. Each of us in the group has had the opportunity to comment on the writing of others and also to have his or her own work constructively criticised. However, special mention needs to go to Di Montague whose energy, enthusiasm and whip cracking skills encouraged us to submit our efforts for final scrutiny and collation. Steve Jacobson has put in many hours further editing and fine tuning the material. Irene Waters and Di have done the hard work of finding and dealing with an appropriate publisher. Jude Hatton has swiftly and expertly formatted the text as a whole.

Sincere thanks to these people who have been so unselfish in giving their time and expertise.

We would like to acknowledge the Gloucester branch of the U3A and its role in bringing our group together.

Moreover, without the generous grant of $2,000 from The Gloucester School of Arts and Cultural Fund, this book would have remained a dream. Thank you to Madeleine Snow who listened to our ideas and from them created the cover for our anthology.

We're not professional writers but amateurs in the real sense of the word. We have enjoyed the journey and learned a great deal in the process – not only about writing – but about ourselves and our capabilities. We hope you enjoy reading this book as much as we've enjoyed compiling it.

(Aboriginal legend tells us that 'Willy Wagtails' listen to conversations and are 'tattle tales' – so if you see a pair of these small birds nearby be careful of what you say – it may be widely broadcast.)

Wag Tales

Paul Gannon

'Hey Cuz – How're you?'

'I'm good, cuz – yesself?'

'Yeah, not too bad. Hey wait a sec – we gotta be quiet.'

'Quiet, why?'

'See that little fella over there with his missus? With the black
and white body and the black tail stickin' up – well he's
jumpin' around lookin' like he's taking no notice of us – but
he's listening hard.'

'What for?'

'Ah, he's listening to us. He's listening for stories. He and his
missus fly back to their nest. They talk over the stories they
hear and then go and tell everybody, anybody they can find.
Next thing your stories are all over the place. Your business,
everybody knows it.'

'Gee cuz, we better be quiet.'

'Yeah, just for a sec and then they'll be gone.'

Let me tell you

Margaret Collett

ND I SAID, Bet, I said you can always count on me it'll go no further and she said Beryl you're an angel I don't know what I'd do without you and I said well you're not going to have to and let me tell you, May, she looked dreadful, just dreadful. I didn't like to say – you know me, I'm not one for giving advice – but I thought to meself she'd better get herself to a doctor soon or she'll be sorry. Doesn't look after herself, does she – not since Ted went. You reckon it's good riddance to bad rubbish? I don't know, I think the devil you know and all that. Anyway, *dreadful* colour she was. And then all of a sudden she started to cry. Well, I tell you May, I didn't know where to look. I mean, there we were in the laundromat, with people around – even one of those women all covered up - you know the ones who marry terrorists. What do you say? You would have let her cry? Well, I don' know, I think it's a bit much meself, out in public like that, so I just said try to pull yourself together, Bet, we've got company. You know, just to get her to stop. And she's not a quiet crier, let me tell you. I don't hold with showing the world what's going on inside like. And would you believe next thing you know that foreign woman in the black dressing gown thing came over and sat down on the other side of her and offered her a hanky – none too clean, I might add. You could have knocked me over with a feather! Well, blow me down if Bet didn't take it and blow her nose on it. I nearly died! You reckon it was probably due for the wash anyway? Well, that's not really what I meant. You never know where things have been do you? She sort of leant into the other lady – who was quite a size, let me tell you, and for a minute there I thought she was moving away from me. I thought this girl doesn't know what she's doing – no, it was no good having her carry on like that – so I got both our baskets and pulled her up. C'mon, Bet I said let's get some fresh air and a cup of tea – that'll make you feel better.

Changing Gear

Steve Jacobson

I THOUGHT THE DRIVING LESSON WAS GOING WELL until my long-suffering father suddenly said: 'For Christ's sake, don't go so fast!' He was getting a bit nervous: maybe he regretted agreeing to teach me. I eased my foot off the accelerator and the huge 1938 Austin 12 slowed down. This was not going to plan. The idea was to save money on professional lessons, but the resultant wear and tear on his nerves, our relationship and the old family car, made the soundness of this debatable.

'You've got too much confidence, lass, you've only been learning for five minutes; just take it easy – please!' I parked the car outside our house and he climbed out wearily, saying, 'I think I'd better find someone else to teach you.'

After church one Sunday and his usual pre-lunch drink at the pub, he arrived home announcing: 'I've just talked to Jack

Smith about driving lessons for you. His son, Kevin, is between jobs and has time on his hands, so I've arranged for him to teach you. He was a driver in the Army.'

The instructor-son turned up as arranged. Mid-twenties, tall, dark, slim, good-looking with a beautiful voice. An improvement on the other local talent, I thought. The village entertainment consisted of five pubs and a tennis court and the available young men who lived locally were mostly sons of landed gentry (out of my league) or local yokels and village tradesmen, none of whom met Pop's standards as suitable boyfriends for me or my sister.

For the first lesson, we set off in the Austin: me, full of unwarranted confidence, he rather quiet. Conversation was limited to 'change gear now' or (most often): 'not so fast' or 'don't forget to use your rear-view mirror'. This continued for a week or two and then gradually he progressed to 'What do you do at weekends?' and then, 'Would you like to come out for a drink one evening?'

So I went, the first of many outings, usually to a pub. The village boasted no cinema, club or restaurant and the nearest town was miles away. So pubs were it and, although I didn't drink much, I enjoyed our outings: he was easy to talk to and fun to be with. Our Saturday routine became driving lessons by day and pub-crawling by night.

But the lessons were abandoned after I failed my first attempt at the Test. My parents must have realised that the instructor/pupil relationship had progressed to something which had more emphasis on the relationship and less on instruction. They suggested professional lessons.

One evening, Kevin told me: 'You know, I was living with a girl until recently.' This was socially daring! The girl was Norwegian, so perhaps that explained it - Scandinavians had a reputation for 'free love'. I should have guessed what was in his mind. He then said: 'Why don't you and I live together?'

I didn't give this serious consideration. 'Oh no, I couldn't possibly do that, my mother wouldn't like it', I said. After a few minutes' silence, he said: 'Well, I suppose we had better get married!'

And so we did.

As the Car Turned into the Driveway

Margaret Collett

A S THE CAR TURNED INTO THE DRIVEWAY, Elsie woke from a snug pocket of dreams. Still holding onto her rug and sitting up really straight, she could see between her parents' shoulders and a little way up the track. The rain out there looked like fireworks coming down, all silvery. It was pretty. But not so the sides of the road where the trees stood like bogey men and it was so very dark beyond. Elsie decided not to look there. Besides, they were nearly at granddad's house. She had tried to bring a picture she'd drawn to give him, but mummy said there was no time for that. It wouldn't have taken long to pull it from under the magnets on the fridge. Everyone seemed cross with her and in a hurry and she couldn't think of what she'd done wrong. Maybe they'd found out about the chocolates she'd taken. Oh, well. She loved her granddad, and looked forward to the whiskery warmth of his hug. Grandma was another thing altogether. If Elsie had known the word 'disapproval' this is the one she would have chosen for the feeling her grandma gave her. As it was, she knew that Grandma's first words were invariably 'Hello, Elsie, go and get yourself cleaned up.' Elsie turned her attention to her parents, silent in the front seats. Daddy had just turned off the radio but his fingers were drumming on the steering wheel. Mummy was doing her hair and then showing the comb to daddy who just shook his head. Why didn't they say anything? She had gone to sleep with their murmuring and the car's hum as a lullaby but things felt different now. Sort of sharp. Mummy started to touch daddy's head but took her hand away. Then she turned and said 'Hello, Else. Did you have a good nap, darling? We're nearly there now. I want you to be especially nice to grandma, all right?'

As the car turned into the driveway, Rhonda shifted to stretch her neck and heard Elsie stir on the back seat. She felt in her handbag for a comb and eased her shoes back on. She offered the comb to Mark but he shook his head. The rain was still coming at the car in long needles and the high beam shone silver on the wet gums looming at the side of the road. Rhonda sighed. This was not going to be easy but it'd be much worse for Mark. It might have been better if she and Elsie had stayed home but Mark had said he needed her and so she came. Rhonda turned and looked at her husband in the unearthly lights of the instrument panel. Their usual spasmodic conversation had dried up half an hour ago. Mark's shoulders were slumped and the business shirt he still wore was rumpled. He hadn't yet taken his tie off but must have loosened it some time during the journey. His hair was messed and that curl at the nape of his neck always woke a tenderness in her. Rhonda reached to touch it but then withdrew her hand. He'd turned the radio off, a sure sign that he needed to concentrate. She saw what looked like a dead fox just ahead and turned to distract her daughter.

As the car turned into the driveway, Flo saw the lights and stood from her watch at the kitchen table. She fiddled with cups and saucers and ripped at a packet of biscuits. When the beam dipped and rose over the cattle grid, she brought the water to the boil again and made a pot of tea, putting on the cosy, still staring through the dark. The rain pattering at the kitchen window was like the tears she couldn't yet cry. She gripped the bench and felt her whole body clench with a heavy grief. Mark had insisted on bringing Rhonda and Elsie when she wanted him to herself – just this once. The child would be tired. And grizzly. Bending awkwardly to change slippers for her decent shoes, she heard the tyres spitting gravel outside. She checked her hair in the hall mirror, smoothed down her dress and stood on the front steps, willing the rain down.

As the car turned into the driveway, Mark turned off the radio which had been playing Ella Fitzgerald's 'Blue Moon'. Elsie must wonder what on earth is going on, he mused, but she didn't seem concerned. Should they have told her? Mark could smell Rhonda's 'L'Air du Temps', a little stale now. He heard his daughter stir in the seat behind him but made no comment. He hadn't been able to speak for the last forty k's. His mind was jammed on one hard thought. The rain was still strafing the car and he drummed his fingers on the steering wheel in a kind of controlled, rhythmic tension which was matched by the sensation of going over the cattle grid. He noticed Rhonda putting on her shoes and getting out the inevitable comb. He shook his head almost before it was offered to him. He saw, out of the corner of his eye, that she had lifted her hand to touch him, but just as quickly withdrew it. He wanted that touch. Needed it. The light was on at the front door and, as he brought the car to a stop on the gravel, he saw his mother standing, spears of rain piercing the golden light around her.

I Think I'll Buy a Sail Boat

Chris Dean

I 'VE COME ACROSS A NUMBER OF COUPLES like us lately, retired early and fit and healthy enough to make the most of it. And apparently it's not uncommon for the man of the house to announce

'I think I'll buy a sail boat'. That leaves women like me and you peering upwards at a very steep learning curve. And if you're in this position you'll soon get used to craning skywards from deep troughs. So, I've jotted down a few pointers I've picked up the hard way and some I've learned about over a conspiratorial glass of white, and I hope they are of some help.

- Time – everything takes longer than he estimates, so allow plenty if you are tagging along. There is no such thing as 'a quick run' or 'out for an hour'. Think ahead to your next meal (at least one) and make sure it's handy. Never make plans for the rest of the day.

- Be prepared – as well as carrying food with you, consider wind shifts, weather changes, unexpected overnight stays. Ever noticed that experienced sailors ALWAYS carry a waterproof bag with them? Inside they have: hat, sunscreen, raincoat, jumper, set of dry clothes, secret stash of munchies. Don't get separated from that bag. It's no good to you in the car or on another boat.

- Apparel – forget the pretty sun frock, strappy stilettos and Melbourne Cup hat. That outfit looked great a few years ago when you were perched, crossed legged at the marina bar, sipping champagne and eyeing off the winch gorillas training on the maxis at Rushcutters' Bay. Be practical because when you get out there it will be wet and windy. Normal conditions would have the shoes confiscated, the hat in the drink, the skirt drenched and flapping around your face in no time. I've seen it happen and it's not a pretty sight. No. Go for coverage. I guarantee, you are better off with the sagging cloth hat attached with cord and toggle, the quick dry shirt and comfortable pants.

- Skipper - Also known as Sir/Captain/Boss or Captain Bligh behind his back. Shouts a lot, makes ALL the decisions, is never wrong, must be obeyed at all times and is very demanding. Punishment for disobedience (and sometimes mishearing or misunderstanding) includes: verbal abuse, banishment and in extreme conditions threats of walking the plank or keelhauling (the personal preference of my skipper).

- Safety – THE most important aspect of sailing. So don't take any slights from the skipper personally because he'll tell you (repeatedly) that he has to be assertive and there is no room for questioning his decisions because of safety. And he has to yell loudly to be heard over the wind in the rigging. He's not really angry with you for throwing the wrong rope, the wrong way, at the wrong time, he's just concerned with safety and he'll forget all about it in a minute so there's no point sulking, he's already planning the next tack.

- Movement – there is a right and wrong way to make any movement on a boat.

  - Initially it's easier to wait until you're told how to enter/exit the dinghy and where/when/how to walk on deck.

- Lots of boat bits move suddenly so always be prepared to duck/slide/lift when ordered.
- Especially be aware of the boom (horizontal pole that holds the big sail down). It is often at head height and can slam from one side of the boat to the other quite unexpectedly causing that 'boom' sound when it makes contact and knocks you overboard (a place you don't want to be unintentionally, though I do have an acquaintance who jumped off a boat once and swam to shore in protest against the skipper).
- Be sure to keep your foot on the outside of that deadly coil of loose rope or you'll be hanging upside down by the ankle with the next wind gust.
- When the wind and seas pick up move carefully and hang on to grab rails (you'll find them automatically when you need them).

- Terminology – it's a whole new language you'll have to learn but here are a few examples to get you started

  - Port : left : red

o Starboard : right : green (somehow these colours and terms mean the opposite depending on whether you're coming or going and even that is debatable at times)

o Sheets : ropes

o Galley : kitchen. Where you are sent after you get the sheets mixed up. It's usually narrow so you can brace yourself with hips and a wide stance in a bucking boat. Don't fill the coffee cups right up or you'll be wearing the contents.

o Berth : bed. Another source of bruises and bumped heads because there's usually not much room and you might have to clamber over something or someone to get in.

Most of it's on-the-job training and you'll soon work out the difference between a jib and a gibe. If you're really keen you could go through that pile of magazines that started on his bedside table but has overflowed onto the floor and collapsed to slide under the bed. When the titles have progressed from 'Trade a Boat' to 'Cruising Helmsman' you'd better crank your lessons up a notch.

There are some good informative articles in those mags and great pics. Take a look at the pictures and envisage yourself in them. I can see you, hanging over the rail with girlish giggles, reaching out toward a pod of dolphins riding the bow wave. I can imagine your excitement at the sudden appearance of your first gentle, inquisitive humpback, pectoral fin raised side on like a faithful dog presenting for a scratch, before she slides smoothly back below the oily surface. Next minute you'll be clutching the rails as she violently breaches up ahead, surging in a high pirouette before a flopping crash, generating a foam of shock waves that vibrate through the soles of your feet to your heart.

It's a captivating feeling, the breeze wafting around you, enticing you with its gentle persuasion, then carrying you at whim to a new enchantment leaving your other world far behind. It's a freedom you'll never imagine till you try it.

So I suggest, when he announces from behind the safety of his morning coffee mug, 'I think I'll buy a sail boat' – just reply 'AYE AYE skipper', knuckle your forehead and go with the flow.

The Black Dress

Judy Farley

'What's a shelf bra?' I asked my friend Sal.

The sales lady, a black widow spider in her basic black, appeared from nowhere.

'Madam does not have to wear a bra with this dress, the support is already there.'

Sal giggled, peered at my chest and said 'Not much to put on the shelf there!'

The lady sniffed and wandered off, looking for more likely customers.

'Why don't you try it on? Sal suggested. 'Every woman should have a little black dress!'

We were doing some serious retail therapy, trying to get the maximum amount of fun and value from our very limited resources. The heavily advertised sales had drawn us in, as intended. The rack had been marked down twice, so its contents didn't really cost all that much.

'What the heck,' I said, heading for the fitting room with the tiny black number tucked under my arm.

'Wow!' Sal was impressed.

I wasn't so sure. It was a bit revealing and I'm not as young as I used to be.

'Pity about the knickers line, you'll need a g-string! I was reading this article in Dolly about the importance of invisible underwear. Just as well you have me to advise you on modern trends!'

'Me! In a g-string! You're kidding. I'm a grandmother!'

'Please buy the dress. Treat yourself for a change. You're always buying stuff for everyone else. It's only $35. If you won't buy it for yourself, I will. Peter will adore it!'

Finally I brought out my credit card and took my purchase to the counter. The lady in black smirked, swiped my card and bagged the dress as quickly as possible.

'I think she wanted to get rid of us!' Sal was grinning broadly as we walked out.

There are times in all our lives when we just want to

break out of the same old mould, to be outrageous and take a small risk. So what happens next is almost predictable. It is our anniversary and I am meeting my husband for dinner, so decide to give him a pleasant surprise. Typically, I've forgotten to buy a g-string. 'What the hell,' I think as I pull my beautiful dress over my head and settle the shelf in place. 'Who needs knickers, anyway?'

It is only a short taxi trip to the restaurant and I am peeking in my mirror when the screeching starts. The braking seems to go on forever and the crash, when it comes, is almost welcome.

His eyes are brown, just like my husband's. 'Welcome back' he says. 'You've been in an accident. My name's Sam. I'm a paramedic. You're going to be alright, but I'm afraid I'm going to have to cut your beautiful dress to put a couple of these electrodes on your chest and another one on your hip. Is that ok with you?'

Futility

Steve Jacobson

You ask me what I think.
I catch my breath, dare I say?
Politely I do try, but hesitate,
am sure I will offend.

Conversation doesn't happen
as it did years ago, easier then.
Cowardly now, I retreat
behind a shield of silence

With you, I have forgotten
how to speak my mind,
I cannot steer that middle course
of diplomacy.

I hope for patience, understanding,
tolerance of my opinions.
But I know these will not come,
I breathe out. Say nothing.

Women's Business

Anonymous

M Y SISTER IS GOING TO PORTUGAL to visit her son-in-law's family. This was the cause of, in her words, 'a painful hour of torture having a leg and bikini wax'. Now why would the one follow the other, you might ask. Her daughters had told her in no uncertain terms that she could not venture out in a bathing costume in Portugal without doing something about her 'wild bush'.

Fortunately, she said, the beautician (if you can call her that) was more or less the same age as her and nearly as unglamorous, so she did not feel too embarrassed. And she was assured that the first time is always the worst and that she should continue with these horrendous treatments, as 'even really old Sheilas do it these days'.

This got me thinking about my own feelings of frumpiness. What I really dislike is entering a David Jones or

Myers store and having to pass the cosmetic counters. I usually try to avoid these areas but sometimes I find myself in all my non-splendour of no make-up, lank hair, daggy clothes and scuffed shoes, amidst the bright displays of lipsticks, eye shadows, foundations, face creams and other 'essential products'. And floating on a cloud of expensive perfume are the beauticians with their perfectly made-up faces, in their immaculate black tight-fitting skirts with shapely black-stockinged legs ending in shiny black stilettos, all looking down their refined noses at me. I creep past trying to hide behind my large Coles green bag with the cabbage falling out the top which I didn't intend to buy but it was on special. My image is mirrored over and over as I blunder here and there looking for the nearest escape.

The only time I voluntarily ventured into this domain was with my more glamorous daughter-in-law whom I had commandeered into helping me look my best for my wedding. Now Fiona is a canny girl who knows the ropes. We approached a beautician and told her my needs. I was then subjected to an hour or so of experimentation with different shades of foundation, eye shadow, mascara, lipstick and nail varnish. I quite enjoyed myself. Then we thanked the lady politely and said we would think about it.

Down the way was a large pharmacy which stocked an extensive range of cosmetics. We matched the colours and came out with the makings for my marriage face at a fraction of the cost.

My good friend Joan, who is ninety-two, also has a problem with the big stores. She went into David Jones a while ago to purchase a bra. Her daughter has been trying for years to persuade her that full armour plating is unnecessary these days, but as Joan says, she feels insecure without this particular undergarment which has been part of her accoutrement for the past seventy-two years.

She was however at a loss when she looked for the underwear department. Nothing on the information board seemed to fit the bill so she finally had to ask for assistance. The very helpful concierge informed her that she needed the 'Intimate Apparel Department'. As Joan says – there is no way that what she was buying could be described as 'intimate apparel'.

While we're on the subject of bras and bosoms, there is my work colleague who sleeps on her back so that her cleavage doesn't get scrunchy wrinkles. I have taken some notice lately of older well-endowed women who wear low cut tops, and sure enough, some do have wrinkled bosoms. Is this because they insist on sleeping on their sides? I'm glad to say that I personally don't have enough bosom to get wrinkled – I think I'll end up like an old lady I used to nurse who described her breasts as 'two fried eggs'.

A visit to the doctor for our two-yearly 'check' is another time of anxiety for women. Have I got matching undies, are my legs and underarms shaved, and how much perfume or body spray shall I spray all over me?

One elderly lady, the story goes, was persuaded by her daughter to front up for her first-ever PAP smear. She got ready at her daughter's house and was soon showered and fresh and off they went. Afterwards on the way home, the daughter asked how it had all gone. 'Oh fine,' was the reply, 'He said I was very well presented.' What a strange thing to say, the daughter thought, so she investigated more. 'I sprayed myself down below with the lovely body freshener stuff in your bathroom,' was the answer. This body freshener turned out to be her granddaughter's glitter spray, which obviously had helped present to the doctor a sparkling display of womanhood.

When I think back on my younger years, I realise that at

times I was so body conscience I missed out on fun things - like being too embarrassed to wear a bathing costume, or the years when I didn't wear pants or jeans as I thought my behind was too big. As I grow older I am more relaxed about how I look - actually that is a decision that has been made for me – my body is doing it all by itself.

I do think that living in a small town helps. We are not confronted by too many very elegant, expensively-dressed women doing the weekly shop at IGA, or at CRT buying up big on cow drench. But we should never let ourselves go completely. So I must remember to put the hair dye on the shopping list and maybe even see whether the nail varnish from that wedding day eight years ago can be thinned out enough to do the fingernails. And is there someone in town who does a cheap Brazilian?

A Great Coat

Paul Gannon

T HE COAT IN THE OLD WARDROBE had bent the dowel rod used to support it. My gentle tug at the coat's hem brought it down on me. I was pressed by its weight into a netherworld of mouldy worn-out shoes and burst leather bags that grumbled softly in retirement on the wardrobe floor.

I hauled it back into the world and was surprised at the hard, nubby wool weave. It felt more like carpet to my cheek than the comfort of wool I had expected. All those nubs: yellows, tans, chocolate brown dyes from the earth and olive greens from the weeds in the wild Irish seas. I fought my way to an air supply from beneath the heavy wool and found the belt was made from the same material as the coat. There were no ragged edges even though it had been cinched countless times to ward off Northern Irish and Scottish winters. The buttons were formed from woven leather, still hard and shiny. The metal buckle covered by the same material as the buttons.

The coat seemed huge to a child like me.

Years later, I thought of my father walking the roads and streets of Britain. Street after street of workers 'row-house' cottages. I had overheard the stories he and his brothers had told of the loneliness of the walk when they had split up and gone on separately in the search for work in those Depression years. I could see my father, his heavy coat reaching down almost to the tops of his newspaper lined shoes.

He would stand, reading that same sign he had read so many times before: 'No Irish Need Apply', signs that disappeared soon after the Nazis invaded Poland.

The coat was cut so that the lapels were flaps that could be buttoned close to the neck, around the ears and up behind the head to meet the obligatory peaked cap. This was a very practical garment and I realised just how serviceable the coat was. Roving workers slept wherever they could, the greatcoat a sleeping bag that did not need to be packed. He could simply lie wherever he stopped and try to sleep in the warmest spot he could find. That was when the full value of the heavy coat revealed itself and it was the same with the hob nailed boots that Dad acquired. No one spoke in detail about how you got those things. You just thanked St Jude for sending them your way, thanked him that you were able to have them. The boots were strong, thick leather - heavy, brutish things that slipped and skittered on the cobbles and uneven paving that seemed to be everywhere. But they did not split and they did not need lining with newspaper that always became sodden and freezing in the constant wet conditions.

The coat was on his back when he first gathered the courage to speak to Peggy. They were both working in black Birmingham making jerry cans for fuel storage as part of the war effort. She became his wife and the mother of his five children. He kept that coat long after the war was over, long after he had any need to tramp the British Isles in search of a job, any job. Then, when he had a home and mouths to feed, and too much work rebuilding Britain, he kept that coat.

We had escaped to Australia, paying full fare on a scow making her last voyage, and jumped the waiting list of those paying a token ten pounds - such was Dad's anxiety to make the change. It meant so much to get away from a country that delivered poverty, depression and war to the new world where kangaroos scattered gold away as they bounded down the eucalypt-lined streets in the sun.

The coat was forgotten, left to hang idle in a dark corner

of an old wardrobe in that bright green and gold place that had no need of its services. I wonder if it reminisced about the days spent travelling on the back of my unemployed father, years before my arrival. It must have felt so alien, this heavy thing designed to harbour warmth in that grey, cold climate where it had come from.

I try to imagine how my father felt when he got home that day with the cicadas thrumming in the heat of the summer afternoon. He would have looked down at his coat laid out on the bed, all the leather buttons fastened, belt secured and sleeves laid neatly at its side. I am sure it would have transported him back to his trudging tramp of Britain and made him glad he had chosen the chance of a new life for his young family in a world that was so different, that offered so much.

He would have hung the greatcoat back safe in its home, with some reflection and something akin to reverence for the garment that represented safety and security when just about everything else had let him down.

Wednesday at Dad's

Dianne Montague

I T'S WEDNESDAY NIGHT and Lynne and I are waiting. He will come at any time now and also wait, outside in the street. Our Dad never comes into our house. He paces up and down, in a cranky way, or that's how it seems. We sit on the wooden window seat in our Nan's bedroom. It can put splinters in your bottom if you slide on it. I want to jump up and down on Nan's big bed until I fall over, but then I won't see if he's coming, so I keep watching. We peek through the curtains, not wanting anyone outside to notice us. There's the front fence and the gate and Pa's roses, standing up in the dark and I see Dad's arrived so we must hurry. We yell out to Mum, 'He's here.' Then out the door we go into the night, our weekly visit to our Dad's.

'Hello Daddy.' I stretch way up to give him a kiss. His big hand holding mine is stained brown and smells of cigarettes. Sometimes I'm allowed to climb onto his knees, then right up his front onto his shoulders, but not tonight. We head off straight away to his house, it's not very far. I'm happy with the walking and chatting, but I don't want to get there. We only talk about what we've been doing at school. Dad wants me to be good at everything and that doesn't often happen. We never mention Mum or our life at home. It's best kept hidden in case it causes trouble. What that trouble is I'm not sure, but I know it's waiting, in the dark to catch me.

We seem to get there too quickly. There's the house looming ahead, with Grandma inside. I take a deep breath and enter. It smells of old and decay and fatty dinner. They have curried sausages a lot. Grandma's powdered cheek comes into view. I guess I'd better kiss it. We sit in the lounge with the radio going, listening to the serials. 'Green Bottle' is on and that private eye show that I'm sure Mum wouldn't want me to listen to. Once again for Grandma, we recite the things that have happened at school. Mum and Dad's wedding photo is in its place on the mantel piece. Mum is in a long, white dress holding onto a huge bunch of flowers. They're both smiling and happy. They look really different now. Mum doesn't have any photos of Dad at home, or not that I know of. Grandma gets us all a cup of tea and a biscuit from a packet. At home Nan makes our biscuits. Most days she has a cup of tea and a tea cake waiting for me when I come home from school.

We've been here for ages and I don't know what to say or do. I hope I don't want to go to the toilet. It's way down the old rickety back ramp. There's no light and I have to go on my own. No one waits by the back door for me like they do at home. The toilet has spiders and I have to wipe myself with newspaper. All the black writing comes off on my fingers. I wonder why they don't buy proper toilet paper? On the way to the back door I pass by Dad's room. He doesn't like us going in there. It's really little, with hardly anything in it except a bed. I saw under his bed once. There were lots of books that had pictures of cowboys and horses on the front.

I feel bored and fidgety just sitting. I'm fidgety because of the fleas. Dad's house is full of fleas. I can see them jumping on my legs but I don't want to squash them because Dad might get upset. The old clock ticks on. Time goes much slower at Dad's. My sister chats away. I wonder if she wants to escape like me. At last Dad's getting up. Grandma's cheek appears again. Out the door we go, into the night. I have to skip along beside Dad to keep up with him. There's my house with its bright lights. Dad bends down to give me a kiss and a hug. He's handing over the usual envelope to my sister. Being two years older she gets to have it. I feel sick. I know there won't be enough money in it and Mum will be mad.

I'm hardly through the door before Mum's racing me into the bathroom. Standing with my arms outstretched, she strips me, throwing my clothes into the bath. Fleas show up on the white enamel. I look at my legs, spotty with bites. I already feel anxious that I will have to go to school looking like this. My sister doesn't have this problem, fleas don't like her. In the morning I will search the bed for any signs of the ones we didn't catch in the bath.

I lie awake wondering why I have to go to Dad's at all. I guess it must have something to do with the money in the envelope.

Wednesday with my children

I'D BETTER NOT BE LATE. They're always waiting for me, peering out the window. I want to knock at the door, but she wouldn't want me inside, their mum, or her parents. About halfway to their house I get nervous which means I smoke a lot. I smoke a lot anyway but it's worse on Wednesday nights. It's just a short walk between our houses and there it is the familiar place, my home for a few years. Harry still has a good hand for gardening, especially the roses. I didn't do any gardening when I lived there, too busy going off to shift work. I hope they're ready. It's really stupid a grown man pacing around out front, but the neighbours know why I'm here. They know all about it. Knew before I did that she was fooling around, but no one was brave enough to tell me.

Here they come, racing down the steps to give me a hug. The little one loves to play that game where she climbs up the front of me onto my shoulders. Giggles like mad she does. They look clean and pretty as usual. I have to give her that, she looks after them well. A real good mum she's turned out to be. Wish she'd been a good wife. Their hands are so tiny in mine, all soft and smooth, with their bright little faces eager to tell me their news. I want them to do well in school, get a good education and a well paid job. They're smart like their mum, not like me. I didn't even finish school. Only work I could get was on the railways. Still, it's been a good job. Always tell me about school, they do, but never about home. Guess they think I wouldn't be interested, with the situation between their mum and me. Probably better that way, then I don't get too upset wanting what I can't have.

Here we are at my place at last. Their Grandma looks

forward to their visit, dresses up for them too. Not a lot to do here, just listen to the radio and have a cup of tea. They seem to be quieter when we get here, probably run out of things to say. Mum goes through all the same questions I asked. Might pick up on something I've missed. The little one looks a bit fidgety, probably misses her mum. Still, it's my right to see them and it's only once a week.

It's hard for me to sit still for this long as well. Lucky I have the smokes to pass the time. There's our wedding photo still sitting up on the mantel piece, been there since the day I arrived back home. I wonder if their mum still has it up at their house. Of course she doesn't, why would she? I just can't seem to take that photo down. Real good looker she was back then. Haven't seen her for such a long while now, I wonder what she looks like?

Is that the time? They're no sooner here than they're gone. Still, I don't know what I'd do with them if they stayed any longer. Couldn't have them sleep here, no room and I'd have to clean up a bit and I know Mum wouldn't want them here. Off we go into the night again.

I'm always relieved when they say goodbye, no more responsibility, but I don't like handing over the money. It was her idea to end the marriage. Why should I have to pay her? Maybe it would be better if I didn't see the kids at all, make life easier. But that would mean it's really over between us.

What Date Did You Say It Was?

Sue Urby

MISERABLE, COLD AND RAINING. It was Monday morning. I'd taken my son to school, but not my daughter. I allowed her to stay home with me as she had a bad cold. The house was far from tidy. The ironing still piled on the board. Breakfast dishes not washed beds not made. That was okay, I wasn't going anywhere and after all it was still before 10 am. These jobs and more would be done but I was tired so today I'd be working at a snail's pace.

Jo-Anne was moving just as slowly as I was, not feeling too good but she made herself comfortable in the lounge room, kneeling, with her schoolbooks spread over the coffee table doing some homework.

I remember asking her what she'd like for dinner. While she was thinking out loud, I shushed her! I heard someone outside the front door. Oh my God! Clearly someone was breaking in. How could sweat be produced so quickly? Instinctively, I ran over to the locked door, pressing both my hands on it, feet apart pushing with all my might, knowing with my weight, I could stop any door from being forced open!

'Who's there? What do you want?'

'It's Sally.'

'WHO?'

'It's Sally from Neighbourhood Watch. It's the 17th. We're having a meeting here. Remember?'

I was silent for five seconds, that's all it took.

'Oh! Sally! Yes. Sorry. Just a minute!' I couldn't believe it. I raced over to the ironing board no I should go and wash the dishes, oh no best I make the beds!

'Jo-anne put your homework away.'

'I'll just finish this Mum.'

'JO-ANNE PICK UP YOUR HOMEWORK AND PUT IT AWAY ... NOW!'

The Signature

Hilary Kite

MY DAD'S SIGNATURE WAS BIG – just like him. It was also bold and beautiful with lots of loops and flourishes. It was carefully executed, usually without hurry, and took up more room than it should have done, often too large for the allotted space on a document.

It seems that it was always a part of my life. I remember my Dad's Signature on notes for school and on the cheques he and my mother wrote out on the kitchen table at the end of each month. They kept the bills on a paper spike on the dresser – the weekly grocery bills from Harry Parr the Grocer, a friend of Dad's from Prisoner of War days and the butcher's bloody edged invoices, stabbed through their middles. There were those from the Florida Shoe Shop and John Orr's, the grand department store in Johannesburg. My mother would sort and add up the figures, checking against the accounts, which had arrived in brown window envelopes.

Dad had a fountain pen which needed to be filled with the dark blue ink bought in a wide necked bottle so that the pen could fit down into the murky depths. A little pump operated to pull the ink up into the rubber bladder. Once the nib was wiped and he had tested it out on one of the brown envelopes, Dad was ready. The cheques were written and finished in a flourish with The Signature.

I imagine a young boy long ago sitting awkwardly at his school desk, always too big for regular furniture. He would scratch out trial signatures on scraps of paper, maybe in the margins of completed homework – experimenting with a sign of himself which would mark him out from other men in years to come. How would he put his stamp on the world – how would others recognise him?

I wonder what ambitions lay behind this almost flamboyant mark? What dreams and visions were captured in this inky stain? Did my Dad sometimes wish to break out from his life of breadwinner, husband and father – restricted by circumstance - to escape into the loops and swirls of his own unexplored desires?

Looking back I realise that I was always proud of my Dad's Signature – it was so dynamic, so unmistakable. I didn't consciously compare it but I knew that it stood out from the rest. My Dad stood out from the rest – in stature, in integrity, in generosity of spirit - all captured in a mark on paper, indelible and lasting.

Silver Brooch

Judy Farley

T HE MAN WEARING WHITE GLOVES lifts me with great care and smiles. Gently he passes his hands across my back and holds me up to the light. My life comes into focus.

I am a small piece of silver jewellery used to decorate the clothing of a Roman noblewoman. She lived, almost 2000 years ago, in Herculaneum, a small city just south of Rome near the Mediterranean Sea. Her spacious adobe villa had panoramic views of the Bay of Naples to the west and Mount Vesuvius to the east. The man of the house was a highly regarded member of the aristocracy with links to the Emperor. His staff were constantly searching for craftsmen to produce gifts to impress his acquaintances. Their marriage had not been blessed with children so he showered his wife with trinkets in an attempt to ease her disappointment in missing the joy shown by many of her friends when discussing their offspring.

I was found in a dusty silversmiths shop near the harbour. That was when my great adventure began. I am crafted from silver. My design is quite simple yet when I am pinned to hold a shawl across a bare shoulder I take on a unique character. I have a small piece of lapis lazuli embedded in my circular clasp. It came from across the sea in Carthage and the intense blue of the stone was a perfect match for my owner's lovely eyes.

On this particular day the weather seemed calm yet there was a haze in the air. Occasionally there would be a slight tremor and growling from the mountain towering nearby. People were a little unsettled, but the mountain often seemed to have a voice and they reassured each other that today was no different. In our household preparations continued for the following day's journey to visit relatives in the north. There were boxes containing clothing and gifts and, of course, jewellery which would be needed to wear to all the social events.

The servant went home to spend the evening with her husband prior to their long period of separation. As she undressed later in the evening she discovered me caught in the tangle of her shawl. She knew that there would be great trouble if her mistress thought I had been stolen, but she would also be punished for not taking enough care of me during the packing. Nervously, she showed me to her husband. Her position with my owner was in danger. Eventually it was decided to hide me in a safe place until her return. Privately her husband thought there may be a reward for me later. I was stored carefully in the upper level of a nearby cistern. The servant knew I would be safe there as the water never reached that level. A decision could be made later about my rediscovery. She returned to her husband's warm bed, her mind more at ease.

Suddenly in the dead of night there was a huge rumbling and then absolute silence. A great cloud of ash rolled over the sleeping town. Nobody had a chance to escape. People suffocated in their beds. My beautiful owner and her devoted husband did not move from their loving embrace. Nearby the serving couple were scarcely aware. Everywhere whole families perished surrounded by their animals as the entire town disappeared under the pall. The inlet to the cistern was plugged with metres of ash.

There I was to remain for 1800 years.

In 1890 when excavations of the area began, archaeologists were amazed by the wealth of artefacts. The cities of Herculaneum and nearby Pompeii were sophisticated with villas, frescoes, public spaces and aqueducts. There were treasures perfectly preserved in the ash which had set like concrete in the intervening years. When the archaeologists reached the cistern I was rediscovered. No one else will ever know who placed me there or why.

Now I have a new home in the Louvre in Paris. Curators carefully clean me regularly and I live under a bank of brilliant white lights. Never again will I be trapped in the dark. The man in the white gloves caresses me again. I have been here now for almost 100 years but I never tire of the admiring glances I receive from the throngs of visitors. When you visit the Boscoreale treasure make sure you look for me.

I will be the most beautiful.

My Grandma's Hanky

Irene Waters

I T WAS IN A BAG OF LINEN I had taken from my grandmother's house after her death. The bag had been carried around by me on my numerous moves and I had never given it more than a cursory look. The day came about a year ago when I finally decided that I would rid myself of all clutter and it was the bag's turn to go. Luckily I decided to go through the contents, just to be sure there was nothing I really had to have.

There were mainly dressing-table doilies of all types. Crocheted, embroidered, lace. You name it, it was there and so was the most exquisite silk handkerchief. It was the size of a man's hanky made in such fragile-looking transparent silk that would never have soaked up any nasal contents. It was a green, a hue that is incredibly beautiful but hard to describe, being neither a forest green nor a lime green nor a lemon green. It was covered in pencil-like drawings that had then been coloured - pictures of ladies and birds and love messages.

What a find! I decided it was a love hanky from World War I. My grandfather had fought in the war. Injuries from it had eventually led to his death. I must have found a hanky that my grandmother had sent to him in the trenches as a reminder of her. It probably had been soaked in her favourite scent and, as he lay there in the stench of war, he could take it from his top pocket and breathe in my grandmother. The hanky even reminded me of her. She had such soft skin, the type you wanted to touch, like a horse's nose. She was under five feet tall and had an air of fragility about her.

With great care I folded the hanky and put it in a plastic bag in my bottom drawer where I keep all my fragile things and there it stayed until the antique valuer came to town. His visit had been organized by the local historical society to give the value, and possibly the history of articles, for a small donation to a charitable cause.

I ate my lunch whilst I waited my turn... It was like Antiques Road Show where the anticipation was palpable. The amazement on the faces of those before me when they found out their treasures' value was as good to see as the treasures themselves.

Finally it was my turn. I unwrapped my hanky and the valuer took it reverently. 'It's beautiful,' he said. 'Do you know its history?' I went through what I had surmised. 'I don't think it is that old,' he said. 'It's so delicate ... it is definitely European. I think it's late 40s, perhaps early 50s. It's a scarf rather than a handkerchief. The type of thing that girls would knot around their throats in rock and roll days. The style of illustration makes me think it must be French in origin.'

At that point I saw a little label I had not seen before sewn into the hem of the article. 'Look,' I cried. 'There's a label!' Before he could see it, I had lifted it up and read, for all the crowd to hear, 'Made in Japan.' You could feel his embarrassment. I could feel my husband's embarrassment, for I had yelled it out for all to hear. I was dismissed very quickly after that. The other article that I had taken was spurned curtly: 'Not worth a penny.'

Even so, I left feeling very happy. Okay, so it wasn't a love hanky but maybe one of my relatives – maybe Auntie Margot – loved dancing as much as I do. I started seeing dance-halls in my mind's eye and, if I ever go to another rock and roll night, I will wear my handkerchief which is once again carefully placed in my bottom drawer.

When You're Smiling

Liz May

'*Good Morning*,' I chirp leaning on the heavy fire door that seals the apartment from the foyer. I need to turn up the volume. '*Hello! I'm here.*'

A small, stooped figure shuffles towards me, trousers baggy on her diminishing frame, wispy hair freshly permed, salt with soft burnished tips. 'Your hair looks nice. Been to Pam's?'

'Oh. It's you,' she mumbles, sounding surprised, not because she wasn't expecting me, she just doesn't hear my approach. '*Are you ready to go? Our appointment (the royal plural) is in half an hour.*' While it's only 3 kilometres, it's an interminably slow progress to launch.

'*Do you have your handbag and glasses? What about your bankbook?*'

As I reach into the third drawer down for the disabled parking permit, she calls, 'Have you got the white thing? Is it cold out? Will I need a jacket? What about a raincoat? They say it might rain. Better put it in. Should go to the loo again, just to make sure.'

I sort through the mail lined up neatly on the sideboard, when her disembodied voice intones, 'There's some letters there for you to look at. Will you pay the phone bill?'

Appearing through the sunroom door, as if she is seeing me for the first time, 'You look nice today. Have you lost weight? That outfit must be slimming.'

'Keys. Where are my keys?' They jangle around her neck as she walks.

'Have you cancelled your meal?'

Lock the door.

Lift down! Doors open, wheels roll, steps - slow and deliberate. Manoeuvre backwards into passenger seat. Load walker, jump in car, reverse, automatic doors grind mechanically. Released into a shiny day!

'It's great to be outside,' she says as we tootle through the quiet suburban streets. No satellite navigation from her today.

Dentist ahead. Damn! No parking in front. U-turn. Park on opposite side of street. Bad move. Spring out of car. Unload walker, get her upright. *'Stay there. Don't try to cross on your own!'* Head down, legs moving robotically, she's off. Slam boot, grab handbag, lock car, sprint to reach her, muttering to myself. She doesn't stop.

'Is there anything coming?' she demands and, without looking, thrusts the walker across the miraculously empty road, up the driveway and into the surgery. Relief.

The dentist trills. She doesn't answer. *'Deaf,'* I say as I proceed to relay the dentist's words in a voice that hopefully won't destroy the hearing of the others in the room.

The dentist smiles with her eyes, above the surgical mask. Mouth agape, impressions are made. 'No eating or drinking for an hour,' instructs the dentist.

That shouldn't be a problem I think, it will take us that long to get out the door. Another visit needed. Another appointment made. Anxious to pay. 'There's nothing to pay today,' the young receptionist repeats.

'Surely I need to pay,' she says, as we trundle down the walkway.

'*Not today!*'

As I shut the door the receptionist smiles.

This time I decide to bring the car to her, but she stands right in the middle of the area where I need to turn. I scrape the wheels on the gutter. 'It's sloping here,' she complains.

'*I know*,' I say.

In the car. '*Where would you like to go now? Gladesville or Top Ryde?*'

'You decide,' she says. Argy bargy, to and fro. Top Ryde. *I* decide.

Park the car. Disabled spot, not far from the doors. 'You could have got a closer one,' she observes as she heads towards the doors. 'Move the car.'

'*Yes*,' I say and dutifully do as I am instructed. Rush to catch her, as she wheels towards the lift - no escalators now after nearly toppling over.

Which floor?'

'*Top. The bank.*'

Handbag rummage. Passbook in hand. Loud voice. 'When will you be back from Gloucester? How much will I get out? A thousand?'

'*Lower your voice,*' I say.

'What?' She continues unabated. 'Don't mumble!'

The teller smiles.

'*Just have to get some make-up,*' I say.

'Good,' she says. 'I need some too.'

'How can I help?' the middle-aged shop assistant enquires.

'I want. It's.... um... oh I can't think.' The words jumble out, slurred and disconnected. 'For my face.'

'*Foundation,*' I prompt.

'Powder,' suggests the assistant hopefully.

'Don't know,' she says. 'What do *you* think?' directed at the assistant, who is blissfully unaware. Locating the compact, the shop assistant, thinking she is being reassuring, says, ' My mother has dementia too. I know what it's like.'

Pointless to explain - Aunt, not mother. '*Not dementia. Just a bad day.*' I say. No one to talk to all day, I think. Who wouldn't be a little stir crazy? The assistant's eyes smile as we leave, compact snug and secure in the walker basket.

'*Where do you want to have lunch? Club?*'

'No,' she says. 'Don't like clubs anymore.' Wander past cafe. 'Let's go to the club,' she announces.

'*Okay,*' I agree.

'I haven't paid my membership,' she mumbles, 'but I'll be okay. They'll let us in.' Confident. I think about arguing, but realise it's futile.

'Perfect park,' she compliments. Things are looking up; lunch special; two courses for $7.50. She insists on paying. Always does.

Drinks on me. Today, she wants wine. Quick quaffs. Too many, too fast. I worry she'll get tipsy. '*Drunk in charge of a walker,*' I joke to her. She laughs. Easy talking. Eats with relish.

'How about a flutter?' Her blue eyes twinkle as she downs the last of the tasteless coffee.

The waiter passes. His eyes search for mine. He smiles.

Cacophony. Bells ringing, tuneless, repetitive notes. Twenty dollars in. Initial reward. Mounts up to thirty dollars. Robotic movement on the button, blank mind. Ten dollars left now. She tries multiple presses, varies the lines played. '*Do you want to go now?'*

'No, may as well play it out.' Tired, she is slipping down off the chair. The wheels stop rolling.

'A lovely day,' she beams as we reach her home. Eyes bright, cheeks flushed.

I smile.

No Mark on the Road

Dianne Montague

NOTHING DIFFERENT HAPPENED AT WORK THAT DAY, just the usual office work. That is until 5.00pm when I received a phone call. 'Is that Mrs Wilson?' 'Yes, it is.' 'Are you married to Mark Wilson from Hobart?' 'Yes, I am.' 'This is Sergeant Mellor, from the Hobart Police. We have been trying to locate you all day. Your husband has been in a car accident on his way to Launceston. He's in intensive care in Launceston Hospital. We think you should go to the hospital as soon as possible.' I don't remember what he said next.

It was Sunday night, nine months into our marriage and our new life in Tasmania. He was leaving the following day to go to Launceston for a week's work, travelling around the State as a pharmaceutical rep. I didn't want him to go but that was nothing new: our love was in its early stages, fresh and intense. He was away every second week, carving his niche in the business world, while I filled in time as a working wife in an unfamiliar place. Monday morning, looking young and ambitious in his suit and tie, he joked that he would have to try to afford a new suit as this one was getting a bit shabby. Neither of us knew where that money would come from. Working hard was not necessarily the passage to wealth. I discovered, at the beginning of our relationship, that he didn't tell the truth about his money situation, or other important things for that matter. It wasn't lying, just making life seem better than it was and I wanted to believe him, so I did. He could do anything in my eyes, I was infatuated. Kissing me goodbye he drove away and I went to my work in the city. Then came the phone call.

I put the phone down. All eyes turned to me when I began to cry and several work mates came over. My boss reassured me that I could leave straight away and they all generously put money in a symbolic hat. I was sure it alleviated the helplessness overwhelming them.

After the initial crying I felt numb but calm. This enabled me to take control of the situation. I rang his sister who lived with her husband and two children, also in Hobart. This was not an easy call to make as Mark and his sister were very close. Back home I packed a bag and rang my Nan in Sydney. She was my surrogate mum, my parents having died when I was a teenager. There wasn't much I could tell her, just that I was driving to Launceston to see if he was still alive. 'I'll ring you when I know,' I said.

We bundled into the car, his sister, brother-in-law and me. Thank goodness he drove. It's not very far from Hobart to Launceston, just two hours, but it seemed like a lifetime. *Will he be alive when I get there?* We said little, just sitting with our own thoughts. The agony was intense. On the way we must have driven over the spot on the road where the accident happened. There was nothing visible to mark it. Looking out into the dark night, I wondered where my life was headed now. I didn't know how I would live without him.

The laminated corridors and chemical smell, familiar to most hospitals, greeted us as we made our way to the Intensive Care Unit. There was a locked door with signs proclaiming that only the chosen could enter. We knocked and peered through the small window in the door. A nurse came and we explained who we were. She let us in. We were the chosen.

The beds lay in rows, each with a body in need of repair. He was somewhere there, alive, but I couldn't pick him out. I followed the nurse to his bedside. Was that my husband? His head was shaven and wrapped in a large bandage and his eyes were closed. The face was so familiar with its dark shadow of stubble but the smell when I kissed him was not. He was on a respirator which had a loud sucking noise. In and out, in and out. The doctor came with concerned eyes and a soft voice. He explained that there was fluid on Mark's brain. When the crash happened he had not been wearing his seat belt so he had slid across the seat and banged his head. That was all, just a bang on the head. It was where he was hit that was the problem. The doctors had to drill holes in his head to release the fluid which had accumulated at the base of his brain and the top of his spine. His suit had been cut open and discarded. I was very worried about how we would find the money to buy him a new suit.

The three of us sat looking at him waiting for a sign. Surely he would wake up. The nurses came and went, checking all the vitals. There was sympathy in their looks and gentleness in their movements. I sat with him while his sister rang their parents now living in Melbourne. Arrangements were made for them to come over to see their only son lying silently.

I slept in a hotel room on my own with the help of sleeping pills. There were advantages in having connections with drug companies. I sat for hours beside him waiting for him to notice me. His family supported each other and me. I cried a bit but mostly I sat dazed. One day, when I was sitting quietly beside him, he coughed. It was his voice alive again! I felt excited. Could this be the sign that he would regain consciousness? It was the only noise he made in a week. The respirator never lost its rhythm. Its sound, always in my head, followed me everywhere.

When we were away from the Hospital, we wandered around Launceston. We could have been tourists, but we weren't. I waited for people to notice that the world was different. 'Why don't they stop their talking and laughing? Surely they know that life has missed a beat. Perhaps I will get some answers in the church,' I reasoned. We attended the Sunday service with all the faithful but the Minister didn't know that I wanted God to answer my prayers. 'Take me God,' I pleaded, 'not my beautiful love, he doesn't deserve to die.' The Minister looked through me and beyond and his sermon left me empty and disillusioned.

After many days and no difference in Mark's condition, it was time to make a choice. The doctors wanted to turn off the respirator, to see if he could breathe on his own. This decision was left to his parents who agreed and it was turned off. I wasn't even part of the process, the decision, or the eventual action. I wasn't allowed to be there. I sat in my room waiting and once again the phone rang with news, this time from Mark's brother-in-law. He told me Mark was dead. 'It's for the best,' he said. 'If he had lived he would have been a vegetable.' I didn't care as I knew I could look after him. Better that than death.

His mum took me to buy a black dress for the funeral. It was a pretty dress, meant for a party. They went home to prepare for their son's funeral in Melbourne and I returned to Hobart. Once again we drove over the spot where the accident had happened. This time I searched for a mark on the road. I didn't see one.

There were hundreds of people at the funeral but I don't remember who they were. There was just a blur of sympathetic looks, tears and hollow words. Once again, I was not included in the preparations or decisions. The coffin slid away and I returned to Hobart without him.

His sister took me in as I couldn't return to the flat where we had lived. It was freezing. I slept with the electric blanket set high all night, missing the warm body that should have been beside me. With the funeral over there was nothing keeping me in Hobart so, saying goodbye to his family I returned to Sydney, back to live with my Nan. Nine months had passed since my departure. I had left to go to a new exciting life and I returned a 22 year old widow. After three months of crying every night, I decided it wouldn't bring him back. I stopped.

Dog God

Paul Gannon

I think I'd rather be by far

more Atavist

than Avatar.

The gods have made

these dogs so good,

better than we ever could.

Gods and dogs have done their bit

it's us that have to learn to fit,

between those balanced animals

and our crazy gods sublime.

Fairgrounds and Fish

Sue Urby

I REMEMBER WHEN THE FAIR CAME to Prestwich Manchester, not just the once but lots of times. They came to Heaton Park and it was an excitement unable to be contained. So many sleeps to go and then you were there, amid noise and people, dogs off leads, lost children with runny noses crying for their mums and dads. Dirty looking stall owners shouting out to you to ride their rides, to win their prizes. It meant having lots of pet fish, not all at once do you see, but one for each time I was there. Walking around the fairground carrying a fish in water in a plastic bag wasn't easy when you still had lots of rides to go on. It must have been hell for the fish!

The noise was deafening and my friends and me would try to shout above it, and when the words didn't reach our ears we'd double up laughing. We walked and ate at the same time, food you could only get at a fair. I can see the lady now, twirling the stick around the inner edges of that tub to collect the fairy floss, and then I'd wear half of it on my face trying to take that first bite, strange really, because you'd take such a big bite yet there was nothing in your mouth. Toffee apples I loved, but once the toffee was gone the apple went in the bin. Hot dogs and pop and then feeling sick... still holding onto that fish.

My mum took me when I was really young. I must have been about nine and I wanted to go on the Waltzers, so we went on together. You'd think the screams we'd heard and the speed they were spinning would have been a hint of what we were to expect. But no! Mum screamed louder than anyone else I'd heard then or since, and not only that, she was screaming to let us off. You wouldn't have heard my screams because my head was buried in my mother's bosom!

Dodgem cars were the funniest, jerking the whole time and looking around to see who it was that crashed into you, and you and that stranger laughing simultaneously. I would never go on the carousels, they shot out to the side far too much for my liking.

When I was older and went with girl friends they wanted

me to go on The Big Wheel. They wouldn't take no for an answer. Waiting in the queue, I kept looking up with that terrible fear of heights, tummy in the worst condition, watching the seats moving to and fro seeing how high the people were. Then it was our turn. Around and around we'd swing, not only the wheel swinging but also the individual seats that from memory were only twenty centimetres deep! Then we stopped, at the very top of the wheel sitting there for what seemed like hours while people were getting off below us. Jenny, seeing my face had turned green and me pleading with her to keep still, made her swing our seat even more. Into the clouds we went with my strange way of thinking that if I didn't breathe, somehow it would help. It didn't of course. Needless to say I've never gone on another Big Wheel.

Down safely on the ground the 'laughing clowns' were fun, fishing for the ducks too but neither won me that teddy bear sitting on the top back row. Many moons later my boyfriend would show off having a go on the shooting range but even he didn't win Big Ted.

No matter how old you were, arriving home was the start of the responsibility of looking after Fleck, my very first fish. Then there was Gold, then Blacky, Sparky, Snoopy. The next one didn't survive long enough to hear its name!

Blood Black

Dianne Montague

'Don't make so much noise. She'll hear us.'

Abby crouched closer to the side of the banister, holding Luke back with her outstretched arm.

'Let me see, let me see,' Luke hissed into the dark.

'Alright, come a bit closer but keep quiet, Mum won't want us to be here. She thinks we're in bed.'

'Where is she? I can't see her.' Luke peered through the rails. The brightly lit hallway appeared to be empty.

'I think she's in the lounge room with Emma. You know how she always makes sure Emma knows what to do, even though she's been minding us for ages. I don't know why she has to get Emma, I'm old enough to look after you.' Abby sat up higher to prove how tall she was for her eight years.

'I don't need looking after, I'm big too. Look.' Luke

proceeded to jump up in the air, stretching up as high as he could, losing his pyjama pants in the process.

'Shush, sit down and be quiet. Mum's leaving soon.'

The knock took them by surprise and they leaned further out to see who it was.

Their mother walked into the hall and opened the door. They could see her sparkly black dress swishing along as she moved. Abby smiled to see her looking so pretty. Since their Dad had left she never got dressed up to go out. Not like she used to with their dad.

A tall man appeared in the hallway. Their Mum pecked him on the cheek and said, 'Come in, I'll just get a coat and let Emma know that we're leaving,' then she disappeared. Abby and Luke held their breath as the man stood quietly waiting. He looked at himself in the mirror on the wall and patted his hair then he walked over to the foot of the stairs and peered up into the darkness. Abby and Luke squashed themselves against the banister, now wanting to be much smaller. Abby could see his eyes searching them out before he turned around and walked back to the door. With a huge sigh she let out the breath that was threatening to burst from her mouth.

'Did he see us?' Luke's face was white and his eyes wide

and bright when Abby turned to speak. 'I don't know, but he's a bit spooky.'

'All done, we can go now.' Mum once again appeared in the hall and the man took her hands with a smile. 'You look beautiful tonight,' he kissed her hands slowly and when he raised his head he briefly looked up into the dark stairway. Abby and Luke jumped up and ran down the hall into Abby's room. They'd seen enough.

Abby woke up and peered around at the dark room. It took a minute for her to remember where she was. Something had woken her. She was sure she had heard a noise. Slipping out of bed she quietly opened the door. A light was on downstairs, she could just see the dim outlines of the hall and the banister. She wondered if Mum was home yet and if Emma had left. Not making a noise, she crept along the hall to the top landing. Someone was talking, a man's voice. Then Mum said something, much louder. Abby slowly made her way down the stairs, and stopped at the door into the Lounge room. Through the small crack she could see Mum in her pretty black dress, talking to someone. She had a worried look on her face and she'd been crying. Then a man stepped in front of her sight. Abby knew it was the same man she had seen in the hall and she didn't like him.

There was a brief scream and Abby saw Mum fall to the floor. She turned and ran out into the hall and up the stairs. She knew that she had to get to her brother's room and hide with him somewhere. They had to get away from that man. Pulling her groggy brother out of bed she held her hand over his mouth to keep him quiet and whispered to him to follow her. Luke knew something very bad was happening otherwise Abby wouldn't look so scared. She opened the door to the cupboard and they both squashed in. At the back was a cubby hole where they often played hide and seek. Abby knew it was well hidden because it had a small door which looked like the back of the cupboard. If they stayed very still that horrible man wouldn't find them.

It was hard to keep quiet and wait. Eventually they heard a small noise and the door to the cupboard opened abruptly. They held their breath, eyes staring at the connecting door expecting it to open. It seemed like ages but finally they heard the door close again. He hadn't found them but Abby knew not to go out yet. She wanted to get to her Mum. Luke started to cry and squeezed tightly onto Abby's hand.

She waited until she couldn't wait any longer and then slowly opened the doors and peered out into Luke's room. No one was there so they made the long journey down the hall to the top of the stairs. It was with a different feeling than earlier that night that they peered down into the hallway. There was still no one around. She'd have to risk it and go downstairs. She wanted Luke to stay at the top but there was no way he'd let go of her hand. They crept downstairs and along to the door leading to the lounge room. It stood ajar as before so they peered through the crack. There was Mum on the floor. They raced into the room. She lay on her side as if asleep, but they could see a red coloured stain on the carpet. It had left a big circle of dark red on her beautiful black dress. Mum won't be able to wear that dress again Abby thought as she shook her Mum to wake her up.

Then a man's voice came from the doorway. 'So there you are. I knew you'd come down eventually.'

Jumping the Gun

Paul Gannon

'G'Day'

'Hello. D'ye mind if I sit there?'

'No. Go for it. This flight to Melbourne's crowded isn't it?'

'It certainly is. Is that your home town?'

'Bleak City! No way. I'm from Sydney. I'm headin' south on business.'

'It's not as bleak as Glasgow, let me tell you.'

'That's your home town? You're a long way from home.'

'Well it hasn't really been home for a long time. I'm an Antipodean now. I have been for some time. I love it here – in Australia that is.'

'I see here in this morning's paper a body has been found

in a hotel room. There's no details about the death – except to say that it is suspicious and it is not suicide.'

'I'm surprised that it has even been written up. It must happen all the time.'

'D'ya think?'

'I'm sure it does. Any details about the murder?'

'They didn't say murder. They just said dead.'

'I just assumed that if they said suspicious, not suicide, that means murder.'

'Fair assumption, I suppose. Geez, where would you start? You know, to investigate somethin' like that.'

'Well, murder is usually carried out by someone who knows the victim. So they say.'

'Yeah. Maybe they put it in the paper because it is not like that. They might want people to come forward or something.'

'That's a point. Mind you, that won't work if it's a professional hit.'

'Well how are they going to tell if it's a professional hit?'

'Probably a bullet hole right where the heart is. And another in the forehead just above the nose. The kill shot.'

'What size hole? Wouldn't there be a mess? What about the noise?'

'Whoah. One question at a time will ye. The hole would be made by a nine millimetre slug. No mess with the right ammo. And a nice quiet 'plop' when the trigger is squeezed.'

'No mess, no fuss, no bother I guess.'

'You've got it.'

'Where do assassins disappear to when they do something like that? And how do they get out – or in for that matter?'

'Well they probably use a Gloch. Nine mill so it does the job first time every time. Twenty twos are good, but you want some real killing power to make absolutely sure.'

'Good grief. How do you carry something like that around with you?'

'Well, they're not heavy. Plastic butt, ceramic barrel and they're not large considering the job they do.'

'You seem to know an awful lot about the subject.'

'I worked for a long time for the Glasgow Police. The school of life!'

'What - did they get involved with professional hit men?'

'Yes, both Sinn Fein and the Loyalists had some very bad boys working for them. Listen to me using past tense when I speak. They're still at it only I'm not directly involved – any more, that is.'

'So, how does this plastic butted, ceramic barrelled Gloch thingo work?'

'Well, you – I mean they, break it into parts and put it into several different places in their carry - on luggage.'

'Why "carry - on"?'

'You don't want to hang around carousels. Less speed, more time hangin' around, the easier you can be detected. In, out, done and gone before anyone knows you've even been in town.'

'Struth. Well what about ammunition. How do you get that in and out.'

'You're in a pistol club. Very fussy about your ammo – so you carry it with you. It's quite legal.'

'Really? I'm surprised.'

'It's not illegal to carry ammunition by itself. It is to carry a loaded weapon on a plane. But of course you haven't got a weapon. You have a tube of ointment and a toothbrush holder or stapler or some such. That's what it looks like on an x-ray.'

So this professional jumps off a 'plane, straight through customs with one little carry bag, goes to the hotel where his target is and two little plops later he's back on a 'plane and outta there.'

'That's it. You're a quick learner. Mind you, you usually jump on a 'plane and get yourself to another city post haste. Break your connection to the spot as soon as possible.'

'So these pros get paid a lot of money for this clean 'wham bam thank you Ma'am' service.'

'Och. There's our call. Time to get on board. Yes, I guess they do. Mind you, governments have not been shy about using the pros to take care of a situation that needs executive action. They're the cases that seem to disappear from view. No media, no police action. Unsolved.'

'Like the one in today's paper?'

'Could be. It'll go quiet in the next few days.'

'Probably done by a pro contracted by a government agency. MI something.'

'I'd say MI6. They would have contracted someone who travels much as we discussed. A retired cop who is still allowed to carry his I.D. and police warrant card. Much like this one I still use, see. Glasgow Police on official business in Australia. No one ever asks what sort of business. If some local official does ask one quick 'phone call sorts it out in a hurry. Mind you, that hasn't happened in a long time. Enjoy your flight to Bleak City.'

Staying Afloat

Lyn Stewart

Barrington, NSW

21st May

DEAR DOROTHY,
How are you my dear? I know you like me to keep you up to date with family doings. Today I have a story for you and in some ways it's lucky I'm still here to tell it. The family had a bit of an adventure Easter Sunday.

You might remember our conversation last Christmas about canoeing on the Barrington River. We all decided it was a good idea so Maggie made the arrangements for a canoe trip for everyone visiting over Easter. That included my brothers Ian and Andy, Ian's son Michael who is now a very grown-up nineteen year old - you wouldn't know him and such a good-looking boy - Maggie's daughter Kirsty and her husband Simon, and my old friend Melba who came up from Newcastle. The hire man had a four-wheel drive and big trailer for the canoes and we followed him in Maggie's car to a ford in the river called Rocky Crossing. We left the towels, and our gear with Maggie: she preferred to do the sisterly backup and meet us at the end. It was then about ten in the morning and we had about a dozen little easy rapids to go down to reach Barrington Bridge about one o'clock. We were all decked out in shorts, T-shirts, sneakers, life jackets and helmets in case we came a cropper and bumped our heads, ho ho. We carried the canoes down to the water's edge. The river is about thirty metres across at that point, and swiftly flowing. The hire man held each canoe as we got in, two to a canoe and Michael in a kayak by himself.

Kirsty and Simon were first off the mark and sped away downstream about twenty metres or so as the water was gushing past. They hung onto an overhanging branch as Andy and Melba went next. They seemed to be OK. Melba was the only one of us with some paddling experience. Michael followed and glided away down-stream out of sight at the first bend. Then Ian and I got into the last canoe and off we went wobbling straight into the main stream. Then over we went! Well it fair took my breath away, and I mean literally. Out of the canoe and gasping for air. Boy is that water cold! Someone yelled 'hang onto your paddles' but I was more preoccupied with gulping for air. Ian lost his glasses but mine were pinned to my face by the helmet, thank God.

The two of us, and the canoe, were carried down stream until we reached calm water. We had to find a spot where we could get up onto the bank, then walk down stream to the canoe. Thankfully Michael became the canoe retriever. I don't know what we would have done without him. But that was just the first of many spills. Every time we arrived at some rapids it was on for one and all. If it wasn't Ian and me getting a dunking it was others, and sometimes all of us. Michael seemed to be the only one who could stay afloat. And he wouldn't swap his kayak with anyone.

After we had swapped paddling partners, Melba and I were swept over to some reeds and stuck fast. We pushed and pulled to try and free the canoe but we just couldn't. The solution, we thought, was for someone else to yank the boat free. Both Ian and Andy were standing on the bank opposite and I shouted for their help. They looked at the task, thought about it - it meant wading across the river - and both of them said 'no way'. Well, we kept on struggling with the reeds but made no progress so someone just *had* to help us. Eventually it was Simon who volunteered. He waded across. The water was moving swiftly and he's not that tall, so it came almost halfway up his chest. But with steady steps and great balance he made it. So brave...my hero forever! He had us out in jiffy and waded back to his own canoe.

Then it was me and Simon in a canoe together when we came to the part of the river the hire man had warned us about. 'A big log is sticking out into the river from the far bank' he had told us. 'Whatever you do don't go near it - it's trouble'. We spotted it on the far bank about twenty metres down from our next rapids. They didn't look too tough so we thought if we lined ourselves up into the best position before entering the fast water we could cruise well clear of the log, no problems. But just as we reached the rapids the canoe swung around and we went down backwards, out of control and over to the log. I tried to push us away but the water was too strong and we got stuck on the upstream side of it. It was jutting out about chest height but do you think we could push our way off and around it? No way José. The more we tried the more stuck we became and the end of the canoe was being pulled down under the tree. We were taking on water and I honestly thought we would drown if we didn't get out of the canoe. So that's what we did on Simon's count of three - fell over the side into the water. The canoe popped free and swept past as we bobbed our way downstream, still clutching our paddles. If you lie on your back with your feet facing down river you can more or less see where you are going and kick yourself around obstacles, fallen tree branches and the like. It's scary but quite manageable really. Simon cut his hand on a rock as he fell out of the canoe but, apart from a few heavy bumps, I was still in one piece.

By the time Michael retrieved our canoe Simon and I were sitting down on a grassy spot resting and watching Ian marching up and down on the opposite bank. He and Andy had fallen out of their canoe - I'm not sure just what happened but there he was doing a rant. You know what a funny man he is. He could have made a living writing for a comedian. He was mad as hell and stomping up and down throwing his arms in the air and saying wild things. 'I'm going to set a Rottweiler on my sister Maggie. What was she doing sending us out on this river in these effing canoes?' We were all laughing at him. How he can be so funny and so mad at the same time I do not know. After a while he sat down and refused to move on.

You get the picture. That's how it went all morning and into the afternoon. Once, when Melba and I were getting back into the boat (yet again) I looked up to see two canoes go past - two adults and two children, one child just five or six years old. Their happy chattering wafted across the water as they slipped past and around the next bend as though they paddled this river every day. *We* were obviously rank amateurs here!

Finally Barrington Bridge appeared and Maggie was there with the canoe man and his trailer. Kirsty had given up earlier once she spotted the road not far from the river. She walked back while Simon paddled the rest of the way. I wish I could end this story like the old school composition – *we went home tired but happy.* But it was not quite like that - more *exhausted, hungry, relieved, bruised, cold, wet,* and for some of us, Ian in particular, *grumpy.* But Melba had me gobsmacked - she said she would be happy to go again!

Well there you go Dorothy. Hope you enjoyed our trip. I know I won't forget it in a hurry.

Love

Lyn

A Costly Tradition

Hilary Kite

T HE EARLY MISTS HAD GIVEN WAY to a bright morning by
the time she had completed her tasks. Just one more
thing to do - but it could wait a short time.

She came out of the dim interior cradling the package.
Sitting down in the doorway, she loosened the tape and let the
paper fall to the ground. Vivid colours of red and green,
purples and blue spilt out into the sunshine. She stroked the
soft pile and brought its silky folds up to her face, the new
fragrance dispelling the pungent odour of death.

'Aai,' she sighed – such a beautiful thing. Such a warm
promise for the cold nights ahead – the icy Highveld winter
nights, when clear star-filled skies would herald sparkling
frosts of dawn.

She stood slowly, and reverently wrapped the blanket
around her thin shoulders. Too warm for this beautiful day, but

she yearned to feel its comfort for a short while. As she turned to sit once again, she saw the money tin, now empty, lying discarded on the mud floor.

'Aai,' she sighed again, remembering the excitement of that day such a short time ago. She had not dared to be late, and had sat long under the large acacia tree, the carefully saved coins knotted heavily in her old headscarf, secure under her clothes. Eventually the bus and the dusty ride into the big town with its big shops.

She had chosen with care, going from one shop to another. Until at last, content, had carried the newspaper-wrapped parcel triumphantly home. This winter she would not be cold.

The wavering, high-pitched funereal ululating broke her reverie. The village women were approaching. The time had come. She rose and putting off her prize, went slowly into the hut where the cold still body lay. Her niece.

She understood the tradition – her best had to be given. But she was so loath.

****

It was her duty - it was done. And, as the hard clods of

brown earth fell onto the small form, now warmed in rainbow softness, with grief and regret, at last the woman wept.

Rebecca

Hilary Kite

REBECCA HAS NO COMPUNCTION about saying things as she sees them. We were all politely munching our decidedly less-than-well-cooked pizzas when she declared in a loud voice, 'This is still raw!' and picking up the paddle proceeded to slide her pizza back into the oven.

My brother-in-law Roland was very proud of his newly built pizza oven on their back patio. He had made the fire inside and stoked the coals. My sister, Renee, had the dough rolled out and toppings all ready and we each assembled our own. Then the cooking began – one custom-made pizza at a time.

Now, the fact of ten people all waiting for their lunch might be the reason that Roland didn't leave the pizzas in long enough, but they certainly were a little on the raw side. No-one was game to say anything. Instead, murmurs of 'wonderful' 'really good' and darted glares at my young sons not to say anything rude.

Rebecca, however, could be relied on to state the obvious and we are all a little afraid of her. I will tell you how she became part of our family and indeed, in many ways, came to rule the roost.

Forty years before my parents moved house. When they went for the final inspection the sellers asked my mother whether she would 'take on the maid'. My mother was reluctant, having planned to just employ a char once a week and had no plans to employ a full time live-in servant.

Up until that time our family had enjoyed the services of Regina Qata who had, over many years become my mother's best friend and confidante. She had come in faithfully each week day from her home in Meadowlands, which in my childish days sounded such a lovely place, but that I later found out was part of greater Soweto, with unsealed dusty roads and tiny square box houses, each on its own patch of bare earth. Regina lived there with her son and we visited her home on occasion. Later on, I would sometimes give her a lift home, a young white girl driving her dad's big car, never thinking myself in any kind of danger. I also drove my mother to visit Regina when she was ill – in the huge Baragwanath hospital in Soweto. And when she died our family mourned and my mother lost a soul mate.

So Mum really wasn't at all disposed to venture into this new relationship – bringing another person into their home. But Rebecca was desperate to keep her job and her room off the back of the garage and my parents of course said 'yes'.

Right from the beginning Rebecca did things her own way – or in the way she had been trained by her previous employer, a very houseproud Italian lady. The parquet wooden floor was polished to within an inch of its life three times a week – something I had the utmost trouble getting Rebecca to stop doing when I lived there for a time with my toddler son who kept on slipping and falling and banging his head. Rebecca worked to a strict routine and woe-betide anyone who ventured to do anything other than washing on Monday or ironing on Tuesday.

But I'm getting ahead of myself. A year or so after employing Rebecca, we realised that this amply proportioned lady was in fact now pregnant. In true African custom she had to prove herself fertile before her boyfriend would consider marriage. Also in true African style once she had had the baby

– a baby girl she named Tracey - the boyfriend disappeared and she was left to rear the child on her own. For a time she kept the baby at my parent's home and we all became enamoured of this little girl. However, once she was a toddler she was sent away to be cared for by her grandmother and aunt who lived in their homeland province 300 kilometres away where Rebecca, who was the only bread winner of the family, was building her own house. She would travel there three or four times a year to visit, or sometimes the aunt would bring Tracey to Johannesburg to see her mother.

A couple of years later my mother died suddenly and my sister and her husband bought the family home. Rebecca has continued to work for them ever since and when they moved across town, she went with them. She has kept the house spick and span, the washing squeaky clean and beautifully ironed, helped to raise their two daughters and has grown larger in size and lost most of her teeth - this last gives her a big gappy smile and a certain lisp, as she refuses to wear her false set.

Malogadi Rebecca Matotola stood together with Roland and Renee in the long lines in 1994 to vote for the first time in her life. She has her own philosophical outlook on politics, claiming that the old South Africa was 'better than nowadays' - being distrustful of the present leaders.

And Tracey? She attended the village school and eventually passed her matriculation. She was accepted into teacher's college but almost inevitably fell pregnant and never graduated. The baby girl, Caroline, came in her turn to be cared for by her grandmother – living with Rebecca in her flat behind Renee's house, but spending a good proportion of her time as part of the family.

Tracey has never had a formal job. She makes a small living by running a spaza shop - selling sweets and small items at the side of the road. She never married but gave birth to a second daughter recently, her mother only learning of the pregnancy just before the birth. Rebecca refuses to look after the second child and only sees Tracey when she comes needing money.

Caroline has had so much more opportunity than her mother and grandmother. She has been brought up in the 'New South Africa', lived in a middle class neighbourhood and attended good schools. She passed her matriculation and is now hoping to find a 'learnership' position which would pay her a low salary and offer her on-the-job training. She probably has no idea of it, but the future hope of the nation lies with such as she.

And Rebecca continues to say things as she sees them. Her house is almost finished but on her last visit home, she was less than happy with the plastering. She told the builder what she thought of his handiwork and fired him.

Having no birth certificate, she cannot prove her age but has always said she was born in 1945. However the authorities have decided that she is five years younger and Rebecca is convinced that this is a ploy to avoid paying her the aged pension.

Rebecca, a unique, frustrating, wonderful woman, full of character and spunk. What could she have achieved in another place at another time?

A Violet Reaction

Steve Jacobson

I T IS GENERALLY AGREED, between the women I call my friends (all of a certain age) that having to buy new bras rates as one of life's least enjoyable shopping experiences. I say, 'having to' because most of us do this only when we absolutely *have to*, when is no life or lift left in the old bras. As my mother used to say, 'You really must get some new ones, dear. What would happen if you got run over by a bus?'

These days we try to think more progressively and imagine, if we took a new lover, what would he think? (We should be so lucky.)

So at last, having summoned the energy (if not the enthusiasm) for the big day, I get as far as the shop, where I am confronted by a huge range: more brands, shapes, sizes, materials and colours than I thought possible, all at exorbitant prices for what are, even in the larger sizes, only small pieces of material, lace and elastic somehow sewn together.

But not all of them are for the likes of me I used to keep the label from my current bras in my wallet so that, next time I shopped, I would know the size and make without the drama of actually trying them on. Unfortunately it is so long between purchases that inevitably I am greeted by 'Oh, that went out of stock ages ago' or 'Well, we used to stock that one but it wasn't very popular'.

Undaunted, I give the sales assistant my size (at least my size at the last measure), my preference for colour, shape, type. I then find that there really isn't *that* much choice: the ones that appeal to me would be suitable only if I were a size 8 or 10. Dream on!

Back in the real world of the fitting room, the curtains of course don't actually close all the way across and the mirror is particularly unflattering and leaves no illusions about my changing figure.

I do the sensible thing and have the new bra 'fitted' by the assistant. This is the one unchanging, almost comforting, aspect of the whole experience. Most of these ladies are thankfully still of a more mature age, usually sympathetic by nature and with special expertise. So at least I am not being served by someone fresh out of high school and young enough to be my granddaughter.

I discard some of my clothes, most of my dignity and certainly all my vanity, and just hope the nice lady won't notice the bulging flesh. Of course she does but she is too polite to comment. After having tried on what seems like half the stock in the place, I eventually find a bra that is comfortable. I look at the price tag and try not to worry about it (after all, it's not something I buy every day) say, 'Yes, that will do,' take two while I'm at it, thank goodness for my credit card, and then go and recover with a coffee (while really preferring something stronger).

I am quite pleased with myself, especially as the shop is having an '*up to 50% discount sale*'. Of course, the 50% didn't apply to the ones that fitted me, but even at 30% off, it's still a saving. It's only when I get home that I'm unhappy. The style isn't too bad, the fit is perfect (well, as near perfect as possible given the shape it has to cope with) but it's the colour I don't like. In fact, it's awful: it's what a friend used to call 'old ladies' colour' – a particularly uninteresting flesh tone. I can never understand why that colour was, and obviously still is, popular with undergarment makers. Is it supposed to blend in with one's flesh, thereby rendering the garment invisible? I think the theory is that the bra won't show through if one wears white. These days it doesn't seem to matter much what shows through.

So I'm a bit annoyed with myself for rushing through the purchase and not giving it more thought. It's too far to travel to take the offending items back, even if I could have exchanged them. Then I think: I could dye them a colour which is more interesting than flesh. I buy a tin of purple dye. Why purple? Well, I don't know, it just appeals. I follow the instructions, prepare the mix, dunk the bras in and, while I'm at it, put in all my old bras as well. And they all come out surprisingly well.

Of course, my husband is completely bewildered by all this, which in itself I find quite delicious. 'Why did you do that?' he asks.

'I don't know, I just felt like it,' I say, which is quite true. I couldn't have explained anyway.

But when I tell my girlfriends (of a certain age, of course) what I've done, they all say 'how wonderful!' None of them asks why - no explanation is needed. One, however, does ask, 'Are you going to dye your knickers to match?'

Now there's a thought….maybe next week……

The Last Shift

Irene Waters

W E WERE SO BORED. Bored and depressed. The government in its wisdom had decided that we were no longer necessary to the community. The hospital was to close. We were past the marches and protests and were in our final death throes. Only a few weeks to go before the doors shut for the last time.

The patients were drying up. Here we were, highly trained intensive care nurses with not a single patient. We were used to running all day. The hospital serviced the North Sydney night club area which gave us our share of stabbings, bottle attacks and motor vehicle accidents, giving us a variety of injuries to deal with. Ours was also a major kidney unit with a transplant team which provided a different kind of excitement. But probably our most intensive long-term patients were complicated aortic aneurysms which often led to multiple systems failure - giving us a real challenge to try and keep them alive.

So we were bored. Not a patient in sight. The ambulances were now taking all casualties to Royal North Shore Hospital, our elective surgery had stopped and this looked like it was going to be the way our shifts would be until we left. My fellow work mate, Judy, and I had chatted all morning. We had tidied and restocked and visited other areas in the hospital. At least they still had some patients. After lunch we waited resignedly for the next shift to come on to relieve us.

'We should check the emergency trolley,' Judy suddenly proclaimed.

'Yes, I guess you never know one of the old nuns might need resuscitating,' I rejoined.

'Hey why don't we make them jealous and make it look like we have had a really busy morning and leave them to clean up the mess?'

'It'd give them something to do at least,' I said as I imagined the night stretching far into the distance. 'Hey I know, why don't we get John the wardsman to be the body and we'll wrap him in a shroud then get the nurse when she comes on duty to take him to the morgue?'

'He could sit up when they're in the lift and scare the living daylight out of her.' We laughed at the image of it. The more we thought about it the more fun we gleaned from it until finally we just had to do it.

We had worked through enough resuscitations to know how to make it look realistic. The wardsmen were as bored as we were and happily agreed to do it. We roped in Tony, one of the resident doctors and had him sitting at the desk writing copious notes and filling in the appropriate forms. By 2.30pm we were prepared, the curtains were pulled hiding the shrouded body behind. The other wardsman was in attendance with the flying dutchman and we looked as though we were trying to tidy up after an emergency by again checking the emergency trolley.

Right on time our third year nurse arrived for her shift along with our replacement RNs. 'Thank heavens it's that time,' Judy told her. 'We've had a hell of a morning.'

'Would you mind taking her to the morgue? We've still got so much to finish off here,' I requested the nurse, knowing she had no choice but to agree. We all assisted moving John from the bed to the morgue trolley and off they went, the plastic doors flapping their departure. We followed at a distance, as we had decided that if it happened in the lift we would miss the nurses' reaction to the sitting up of the body. It was therefore timed to happen whilst waiting for the lift. We were not disappointed.

At the lift John slowly sat - a mummy come to life. Our nurse ran for *hers*, turning paler than white and letting out a blood-curdling scream. At that point we felt just a little bit guilty. We did get a reprimand from higher up but it was minor. I think they knew morale was so low that anything to buoy it up for even a short time was accepted and the hospital staff had laughed, with the exception of our nurse.

The next day however we were sobered. John had worked his last shift. He had killed himself overnight. I could not get out of my head that I was responsible. Had I given him the idea or had he found it peaceful inside that shroud somehow? I will never know. I will always wonder.

A Long Lunch

Judy Farley

THREE MIDDLE-AGED WOMEN sit at a table, empty plates and wineglasses before them. The restaurant overlooks the harbour and the water glitters with a thousand gems. One yawns, not from tiredness or boredom, but with contentment.

'Do you know, we haven't had a weekend away like this since we finished school?' *Oh, no! Not Memory Lane this early in the day!*

Thoughts of their teenage years push everything else out of their minds, and the reminiscences begin.

'Remember that school dance where we took all the extra make-up with us so we could look like ... what was that girl's name ... you know the one we thought was a bit wild ... Marilyn something ... yeah, her. Your mother went really mad when she had to try to get the makeup out of the pillow cases next day, didn't she?'

'You know, Marilyn wasn't all that bad. I worked with her in Brisbane a couple of years later. Maybe she just grew up a bit quicker than we did.' *Well, she grew out, anyway! She was certainly well-endowed. How I hated her for that*!

'Do you remember the year we all fell in love for the first time?'

'Ooh, yes. Pity the guy didn't know we existed.'

'He must have been blind not to notice us blushing and stammering around him.'

'How embarrassing! He was kind of cute, though. I wonder if anyone ever caught him?'

'I don't think so. I see his mother at work sometimes and I'm sure she would have told me.'

A man at the neighbouring table looked up as their laughter rippled around the room.

'Shhhh. You'll have us thrown out of here.'

'My first husband ... ' the oldest woman begins. The other two roll their eyes. *The guy had been an alcoholic loser and she only ever talked about him after the second glass of wine.* '... always maintained he had caught me on the rebound from someone.'

'If he only knew how right he was.'

'Mmmmm.'

'Your second husband is a much better deal.' *He's a bit boring, still not really good enough but I can't tell her that. We've been friends too long for such honesty.*

The younger woman glances at them both, colours slightly and says, 'At least you can compare them. Do you ever call out the wrong name in a moment of ecstasy?'

'Of course not. There haven't been that many! I mean, husbands, not moments of ecstasy!'

Their laughter is more of a roar now. Their neighbours have stopped chatting and seem to have more than a passing interest in their conversation. *These women look so respectable and they seem to be talking about SEX!*

'I'm really happy I'm single. I'm too set in my ways now to be able to share a home with someone else.' *Sure. They both know how many years it has taken her to get over Andy, that two-timing married guy. He had been going to leave his wife, but the kids were the problem, and then she had made all sorts of threats about telling his boss and the marriage maybe wasn't all that bad after all. Blah! Blah! We would both love to make him realise how his indecisiveness almost destroyed her.*

The opportunity may still arise.

'Sometimes I'd love to be single, not having to consider anyone else. Does that sound weird?'

'No. I think we're all a bit like that at times.' *Sounds as though things are a bit dicey there. As suspected. Better not let on though.*

'Will we order another bottle? None of us is driving.'

'Sounds good.' *Hope I can stagger up the steps without stumbling! I wonder if she has a bit of a drinking problem? Maybe those long lonely nights ...*

'How are your kids getting on?' *Why did I say that? Prepare for a long dissertation on the wonder children and grandchildren.*

'They are really good, earning too much money of course, ha ha. Grandchildren are growing up too fast. We'll see them next week.' *Maybe her daughter-in-law will have come back home by then. Hope her concerns about their marriage are baseless.*

'How about your family?' *Why am I doing this? We all adore our own, but it seems a bit trivial to anyone else.*

'Oh, they're good too. I can't believe how fast the years

have gone! Those babies are all grown up.' *Oh, oh. Not the maudlin angle, the, 'what have I done with my life' sort of thing. Better not refill your glass!*

'Are you going to share those bubbles?' *Oh dear, wasn't quick enough.*

'Pass your glass. Anyone interested in the dessert menu? ...Waiter.' *If I eat anything else, I'll need to undo the top button on these pants. Where do they put it all!*

'I guess a small Crême Brulée wouldn't hurt. Something to go with the last of these bubbles.' *Is that a small slur in her voice? Surely they're not getting ... you know ... well ... a little bit tipsy?*

'I think I'll need a little snooze this arvo.' *Never could hold her grog, even at school that time they pinched the bottle of Porphyry Pearl. It had been warm and sticky-sweet and they had all been forced to pretend they had a tummy bug next morning!*

'Oh, it's already 4.30! What time are we going to the movies?'

'Maybe we should do that tomorrow morning, we don't need to leave too early, do we? I don't want to miss out on seeing that dishy Colin Firth!' *Colin who? Oh yes, the guy in*

Pride and Prejudice. Ooh, yes please. He's certainly worth a look!

'Now how are we going to divide up this bill?'

'WAITER!'

A Pair of Shoes

Margaret Collett

T HERE WERE SOME FADED UMBRELLAS on the hotel terrace. Louise and Trish headed for the shade of these and slumped onto chairs, dumping their cameras and hats on the cracked tiles.

'God, I'm sick of this hotel. Call this a holiday! Half the time spent swatting the filthy flies away, and the other half pushing away those useless, stinking beggars. I don't know what's worse – flies or hangabouts – I mean, how can they allow them to hassle people like us?'

Trish, used to such outbursts, looked out over the rooftops and at the sunset that seemed embarrassed to be gathering colour through the dust of the early evening.

'Oh, I don't know, Lou, think of all the wildlife we've seen. Anyway, try to keep your voice down, the drink boy's coming with our orders.'

'Drink boy, schmink boy. He doesn't understand a word we're saying, does he, you smarmy sycophant? How did we end up staying at this third rate dump? This drink's luke warm. I'm sending it back. Hey, whatever your name is. This drink …'

'His name's Denton, Lou. It says so on his badge. I think he understands more than you give him credit for. And to answer your question, you said you wanted to save.'

'Denton! What sort of a name is that for a waiter, and a black one at that! This drink is not cold. Not good. You fetch more. Better one. You understand. More drink.' 'Yes madam. Very good, madam.'

Denton was working at the hotel during his uni holidays. The hours suited him and the tips were usually good, although he didn't hold out much hope for this guest, he thought wryly. In his second year of a business degree, he did have some common ground with Louise, and could see how the hotel needed someone with better management skills and some money. He couldn't help seeing himself as the owner of such an establishment – why not this one – in ten years' time. He could work and wait. He was particularly good at the latter.

'Very good, madam,' he repeated.

He found it strangely comforting to repeat this mantra to such customers although this one had just about worn him down over the last four days. He seemed to score her every shift, and her complaints and whining were becoming more operatic each evening. He knew Selina, the room service maid, had been reduced to tears by Louise because she dropped the toilet rolls on the bathroom floor. As if they'd break.

And now, here she was again, making a fool of herself, with that too mild-mannered friend of hers just sitting there murmuring her embarrassment. Usually, he quite enjoyed listening to the rubbish and supplying the odd 'Yes, madam, no, madam.' But tonight, she was really getting under his skin (and he laughed inwardly at his own joke). He took the drink to the kitchen and stuck it in the fridge while he fixed up a couple of other orders. Then, returning, he set the cocktail on the sink and gave it a quick squirt of vinegar from the shelf above. He placed it in front of Louise with a degree of deference that took her aback, and then resumed his position near the door. She made no response for several minutes, and then -

'Hey, boy! Get me another one of those. That was better. Why couldn't you do that the first time?'

'Yes, madam. Very good, madam.'

Two hours and quite a few drinks later, Denton had heard the entire litany. Botswana was a hole. The weather was lousy. The hotels were filthy dumps. The people were stupid, smelly and lazy. It was dark before the pair prepared to leave and, as she rose, Louise stumbled.

Without thinking, Denton stepped forward to steady her.

'Gedyourhandsoffme!' she slurred, 'I don't need your help. Trish! Over here.'

In the doorway, Louise turned.

'On second thoughts, Den – ton my man, there is something. I've got crap all over my hiking boots – from walking around this filthy place. Here. Get them cleaned up and leave them outside my room. Thank God we're out of here tomorrow.'

She fumbled to get the boots off as Trish held her awkwardly. Denton made no move to help. She kicked them in his direction and left.

Denton picked up the shoes by the laces, and holding them away from his body, took them through the kitchen and outside to the bin area where he hosed them down until they were thoroughly soaked. Passing the kitchen again, he saw, out of the corner of his eye, a paring knife.

A stitch here and there would do. It might be days before they fell apart. But fall apart they would. His task finished, Denton placed the shoes almost reverently outside Louise's room.

'Yes madam. Very good, madam.'

Mr Platitude

Lyn Stewart

You stand there hands on hips, you think you know everything.

Women drivers you say, but we're not sinking ships to your

loose lips,

nor distressed damsels to your heroic white charger at ten-to-

the-gallon.

You just take others' words - you steal rather than beg or

borrow.

You think you go with the flow but that's a self-deception.

For you, Jack my dull boy, a bit of hard word-work wouldn't

hurt.

Cream always rises but your talent is beyond the pale.

You're off latitude with your platitudes -

I've plumbed you to the depths of your shallowness.

Get a life!

Old House

Judy Farley

A LWAYS KNOWN AS THE OLD HOUSE, certainly much older than me, it was perched atop a small rise just out of reach of the highest flood level. The long gone family who had built it had studied the lie of the land very carefully. I was not allowed to go too near, probably because of the vermin, both seen and unseen, which must surely inhabit such a place. It was used to store hay in the years before the new hayshed was built. Things had always been hard on the land, and improvements such as dams and sheds had to be saved for. Just when there was almost enough in the bank, the weather would turn and the wish list would be cast aside for another year.

Had there ever been a garden? It had only been used as a place to camp in recent years, but I think a family must have lived there at some time, parents with a couple of children. Every spring there were clumps of snowdrops and the wild river peach trees were covered in soft pink blossoms. These promised a crop of tiny woody fruit to be stewed with generous amounts of sugar. There was also the tangled mess of a bush lemon tree and an orange tree which bore fruit for many years after the demise of the house.

There were three rooms, a kitchen, a bedroom and a verandah on the back. The water was fetched from the river in the early days, lugged up the slippery bank sloshing over the woman's trousers and boots. She had given up wearing a skirt; it had always been in the way and usually hitched into her belt anyway. She was responsible for most of the heavy jobs around the house, not because her man was lazy, but he was out working, gone from dawn to dusk with a couple of slabs of bread and dripping with a bit of corn meat from a recently killed beast. He carried a billy, a tin cup and bottles of tea leaves and sugar tied up in a hessian bag. While he was away from home ring-barking trees or working for one of the neighbours, she battled on all day, dealing with whatever nature and the children had in store for her.

The shady river bank was a welcome respite from the relentless summer heat. How she longed to remove her heavy work clothes and have a forbidden swim in the dark depths. Instead she had to make do with a tin dish and a rough flannel cloth to free herself from the day's sweat. The children had the luxury of an old tin bath, used on the verandah during most of the year, although they were allowed to have the warmth from the fire in the winter months.

Her days were monotonous, working until she could barely stand, ending with the preparation of tomorrow's bread. The weevils in the flour were a problem, until she began to store it in an empty kerosene tin. Keeping the fire going was difficult, especially in the wet weather. The fireplace at the end of the kitchen was made of beaten out tins, roughly joined together. It was certainly not weatherproof. When the rain pelted in from the south on those endless wintry days, the chimney would not draw properly and the fire would come perilously close to dying. If it did, the cycle started all over again, and she had to use the sticks soaked in kerosene to coax flames back, keeping the water constantly on the boil and cooking that night's dinner.

The westerly winds howled through every space during August, and the house often filled with smoke, forcing the family out the door, gasping for fresh air. The vertical timber in the walls had shrunk, leaving a gap which was almost impossible to plug. As in most homes, the easiest and cheapest way to deal with the problem was wallpaper. Glue was made from flour and water then newspaper was applied over the top. It worked well and the layering could continue as long as the paper lasted. It was decorative and there was always something to read in the light of the flickering lamp.

Every couple of months she caught a lift on the mail truck into town and returned the next day with bags of flour and sugar, occasionally some cloth for a new pair of trousers for each of them and maybe some ticking to cover a new mattress she was stuffing with horsehair or bracken fern. On rare occasions there would be a visitor, usually a relative, trying to relieve the boredom for them all, arriving with small gifts. Sometimes there would be sweet-smelling soap for the lady of the house or perhaps pipe tobacco, toys or, most-treasured of all, books.

As the years passed the children grew up and moved far away for work. The man died suddenly at the relatively young age of sixty and the woman was forced to live with her sister in town. She never returned to her old home after my parents bought the property in the 1950s. It was a sad day when the old house was eventually demolished. I had always enjoyed 'reading the walls' and thinking about the barely remembered family who had lived there.

Moon Drum

Paul Gannon

'Ah there Tom, sure it's a beautiful evening.' Tom could clearly see Sean's smile even in the twilight.

'Sure is, Sean- what're you up to?'

'Smokin' this 'ere pipe, sippin' this 'ere brew an' starin' at that big pink moon that just popped outta that hill.' Sean nodded at the rising moon.

'Geez, it's different, isn't it?'

'Best I've seen in a long time an' I check it out every night. Should be good for a few loony activities.' Sean chuckled knowingly.

'So, what have you got planned for tonight?' Tom was not surprised at anything Sean said.

'I'm still makin' me bodhrans and I've got work to do tonight.'

'Really? I woulda thought you'd supplied all the Irish and Celtic bands in the world by now.'

'Dere still buyin ' 'em – probly beltin' the bejeesus out of 'em.'

'It'd take a lot to beat 'em to death.'

'Sure, dat it would, dat it would. Let's see now.' He squinted and looked up to his left.

'I tink just about everyone dat's toured here has got one a dem.'

'All made by you in this little corner of the world? How d'ya get 'em out of the country?'

'Ah quarantine is a thing to deal with comin' in. It's not so hard goin' out. They just carry 'em out as one of dere instruments. The authorities assume they brought it in with 'em.'

They talked for a while about life in the small village, how it was the same whether you were in Ireland or where they were now, in rural Australia.

'I can see where you get the wood for the frame, but what about the skins?'

'Well it's partic'lar, it has to resonate properly and we've talked about the hidin' dey has to take.'

'I can understand that, so what sort of hide is it?'

'Ah c'mon now Tom, don't wanna give away any trade secrets, do I?'

'I can't see me diversifying into bodhrans. I play guitar.'

'Hmm-tell me are you an' your kids animal lovers?'

'You know we are - just look at all the animals on our place.'

'Yez a' got dogs, horses, chickens-what else?'

'The kids bring home rabbits sometimes, the occasional guinea pig, that's about it.'

'Come on.' Sean set off around the back to his shed, puffing furiously on his pipe. Tom caught up with him as he disappeared inside. The fluoros flickered on. He reappeared with a powerful portable torch in his hand.

'Over here.' He took a few steps towards the rear of the shed, Tom following. A click and the area was bright as day. Several hides stretched on frames hung on the corrugated iron wall. Tom could just see some black and orange hair protruding from one of the frames.

'Dere dey are. An' dey'll all sound just right, I can assure 'ya.'

'Where did they all come from?'

'The tip, Tom - the tip! Dat's where they start dere huntin'.

'But how d'ya get 'em?'

'Wid me trusty old twenny-two. I'm sure to shoot 'em in de back o' dere head. I need a nice neat pelt. I show mercy, I'm not a cruel man.

'Sean, that looks an awful lot like Mrs. Carter's tortoiseshell cat to me.'

'Maybe, I only trap 'em at the tip - that's where dey been huntin' ... One bullet to the head.'

'Do these musos know they're playin' a dead cat from our local tip, I wonder?'

'D'ya know- you're de first dat's asked. I'm sure dey'd be chuffed to know dere doin' dere bit to protect Aussie wildlife, doncha reckon? Look at that big red moon. Comin' up the tip to clean em' up? Mind ye there's one thing that gets to me some – when those bands play dere drums they'll hear that sad yowl of a feral cat maybe just a tad.'

The Only Real People

Paul Gannon

Too often we big folk lose our child-bright view,

and forget we can be a hundred years rich,

if we stop and poke in a pile that a few

crazy, greedy big folk like we,

have left as a sign for us to heed.

We don't know any more the load is finger-light,

and all can be anything we ask it to be.

That all we meet can be near and dear

in minutes or less

To be rich or poor,

to love or take fright

is something inside you (and me).

And none of us need have any real fear

if we just be the child that is us.

It was early morning when I asked the warden on duty at the Denver youth hostel to show me any information he had about walking trails. He smiled to himself and spread a map the size of a double bed sheet out on the reception desk.

'The yellow lines are walking trails.'

I looked at the huge map totally crazed with yellow.

'Struth – could you recommend one or two?'

'Well, if I was new to the area – your accent's a bit of a giveaway – I'd go and do the lakes walk. Near Aspen, see the lakes on the map there.'

I had been enjoying the area while it was quiet out of the ski season and had learned the value of the honour system camping grounds set up by the U.S. Forests Department. The appearance of its logo near several of the lakes convinced me that it was the right area for me to camp for the next few days. My sad old station wagon was soon on the way to Aspen.

The country was much more than the topographical maps had indicated. The skiers who had only seen the forests asleep under the omnipresent soft snow doona were missing an entirely different travel experience. I was soon out of the car and the clean air made me want to walk. It was still an almost silent journey with the shoosh of the snow under skis replaced by the crunch of twig and pine needle underfoot. The glare of the white blanket had become a series of sunlight flashes from the mirror ball of the lakes in the background. The solitude of the walk refreshed my spirit and caused a deep meditation. It was Zen and the art of a mountain walk that had to be trodden to be understood.

The faint sound of laughter and the tinkling of children's conversation ahead broke into my reverie as I started on the way back to my car some distance from the lakes. As I came around a bend in the trail cut through the forest, I could see two young boys bending over peering at something on the forest floor. Their amazement was infectious. Like the child in most adults I was instantly curious at their entertainment. I called out from some distance (I didn't want to alarm the budding botanists):

'G'day, What've you found there?'

'Hi.' They said unanimously. 'It's a bug with a million legs!' said one, spreading his arms wide to demonstrate the many legs on his discovery since words had failed him. I was impressed - his words had served him well. I certainly wanted to see his million - legged bug.

'Can I see him?'

'Sure.' They were speaking as one again.

'I think he might be called a centipede.'

'Why?' the inevitable question.

'Cause he's got a hundred legs - 'cent' means a hundred, 'pede' means legs.' The boys seemed not to notice my answer. Their eyes were intent on me, however.

'You talk funny.'

'I just sound funny to you 'cause I'm not from Colorado. I'm not even from America.'

'Yeah? Where you from?'

'Australia.'

'Where's Stralia?'

We started to walk away from the lake along the trail towards where I assumed their parents would be. As we walked we talked about the important things of the world like why I talked funny and how we spoke the same language only different. That led into history and the War of Independence and the history of Australia. We were deep in conversation and the boys had quite naturally slipped their tiny hands into mine as we became engrossed in our conversation.

We rounded a bend in the trail and off to the left gleamed a sparkling pile of iron pyrites. Six year old Sam was goggle-eyed as he gazed at the tailings shining in the afternoon sun. He sprinted toward the mountain of gold, ran to the top and grabbed as much as he could in each hand, held his arms out like a new world champion and roared as loud as his child lungs could manage:

'I'm a hundred years' rich!'

His mate, commonly known as Bud, joined him and repeated the performance. I was taking great delight in the shared glory of Colorado's youngest millionaires. As far as these magnates were concerned it was there for one and all. We were rich in the latest imminent gold rush. There was so much. As we gathered some of our gold and made a mental note of where to return and stake our claim, Sam asked:

'Can I carry your pack?' The Australian flag and the general travel-soiled nature of my day pack appealed to him in some indefinable way.

'Sure you can. It's not too big and heavy?' I adjusted the straps.

The little boy slipped it over his shoulders. It hung down to the back of his legs.

'It's finger light!' I had consumed my lunch of trail mix and my water bottle was now empty. I was amused at the way he described a feather that could be carried with one finger. We started to walk with the pack bouncing behind Sam.

We were making a reasonable pace when I noticed two women ahead standing, obviously waiting for their two boys to catch up.

'Hey Mom, this is Tom – he talks funny!' roared Bud as he ran to his mother.

I could see the horrified expression on the mothers' faces as their minds raced. The last thing they expected to hear was their boys introducing them to a stranger they had found on a walking trail in this remote wilderness.

I assured them that I understood that the boy's mothers were only a small way ahead and the boys and I had only just met and we had travelled the world in the last five minutes. Why didn't I join them and we could all walk together? We spent a wonderful afternoon making bows and arrows and when I was invited to make camp in the same area I accepted readily. We adults had joined the boys in their adventurous fun.

The mother of one of the boys disappeared and returned

with some supplies for the evening meal. After the boys went to bed with their newly made archery equipment close by, the adults turned the conversation to issues of parenting, the loneliness of raising a child on your own. I was shocked to discover that I had spent more time with the two young boys than their own fathers had in the last year. A high point of the campfire discussion was the delight that the women had found in their heli–skiing trips. I could only imagine the joy of skiing in the floodlight of a full moon after being taken to the starting point by helicopter.

We said goodbye after enjoying a long breakfast the next morning. Bud's mother made her way over to where I had camped and asked if I would like to take care of my laundry at her house. One look in her sad sea–green eyes told me that this was not just an invitation to take care of a need for a backpacker on the road. My mind raced through the reasons why I was on my own. The solitude had become a great friend. It would be over one day but not yet. I still had some distance to travel. I declined the invitation as graciously as I could. A lonely mother nodded in agreement with my decision to keep moving. Her head motioned yes but the rest of her said no. She handed me a piece of paper with her contact details on it, smiled a flat smile and walked away.

Against the Grain

Liz May

I T WAS THE SCHOOL CONCERT, an annual event, which drew the year to a suitable close. Each class, beginning with Kindergarten, would provide an item, usually an all-singing all-dancing fanfare displaying the 'enormous' talent pool in the school. The evening culminated in the obligatory nativity play where there was much controversy over who would assume the coveted roles of Mary and Joseph - these being usually assigned to the most beautiful children of the most influential members of the school community.

I was in Third Class and having started school at the age of 4 years and 1 month was at least 12 months younger than my classmates. We were performing a gypsy dance, resplendent in crisp, white ruffled blouses atop full, multi-coloured skirts and adorned with clunky fake silver jewels. I was the very epitome of a Romany - white skinned, strawberry blonde, freckled countenance and chubby.

Our concerts were held in the school hall, a large wooden structure at the edge of the school grounds, which was most well known as the venue for Housie on Friday nights - source of revenue for the church and school communities.

For the students the Hall had another attraction. Each day, compulsory milk was delivered to the school to improve the physical condition of the youth of Australia. A government initiative, it was popular with the politicians, mildly welcomed by the parents and abhorred by the children. The problem was that in summer the milk was delivered early in the day and sat in the scorching sun until the 11am playtime when we were forced to consume the warm, stomach- churning contents. Fortunately for us there was a gap in the bitumen abutting the Hall and this hole provided a welcome receptacle for our milk.

The Hall had a most magnificent polished floor and was a constant invitation to all children to practise their sliding abilities. This, of course, was verboten by the nuns who ran the school with wills of iron and canes at the ready.

It was after the concert had concluded and the packing up was just beginning that the allure of the highly polished floor finally overcame me. I set off down the hall in my socks (for extra slipperiness), chains flying, skirt bouncing beautifully, buoyed by the rope petticoat that was the latest fashion statement in 1957. Skidding halt, quick about turn, and off to repeat the manoeuvre. Coast clear, I launched myself down the hall. In mid flight a black and white shape loomed before me in the doorway, upsetting my equilibrium and causing me to complete my slide on my derriere, almost colliding with my nemesis!

Oh the indignity! There I lay, legs in the air, prostrate at the feet of the nun. It was then that I realised that something was afoot, or more accurately 'abum', discovering that a large piece of a wonderful floorboard was lodged in my backside. I was escorted to the nuns' lunchroom, where I was obliged to drop my undies while my father, who had been summoned, extricated the object in full view of the nuns and whoever else felt that this would be a suitable end to an entertaining evening. It seemed as if the whole world was crammed into that little lunchroom, whose hallowed interior I had been desperate to visit, but not that desperate!

Escher Drawing - Padlock

Margaret Collett

'But I fear it is too late,' said the old man. 'I have left my heart outside the gate for so long. It is chained there, for all to see my pain and pity me. The chains are heavy and rusted. They do not shift or clank, even in the strongest wind. Everyone will know if I move to help myself because of the heavy scrape of chain on chain. They will come to laugh, for it has been many years since I have made use of my heart. I am certain that if I try, I will be too clumsy with fear. When, in the dark of last night, I fumbled through the bars, my fingers found only a padlock without a key. All was cold and hard and, withdrawing my hand, I felt a rough rust which in the daylight was the colour of dried blood. Even had there been a key, the gate to the world is so bound that there is now no hope for me.'

'It is simple,' was the reply. 'You must put your hand through the bars in full view of whoever is there watching. Ignore their scorn. Take no note of their jeers. You must grasp the padlock. It will be glacier-cold. But you must hold and hold until the cold becomes wet, until you feel drops running down your wrist. You will look to see that your hand is empty, but your heart is full.'

Where to Pull Over

Dianne Montague

I KNOW HE'S SICK, but I hate driving. Now he's asleep. I always feel guilty when I fall asleep when he's driving, but not him. Seat pushed right back, reclining at ease. Poor thing, I'm so mean to him. We didn't get much sleep last night. Late night partying and an early morning start to Sydney don't mix. Five hours sleep, I hope I stay awake. Brief look, he's relaxed, eyes closed, breathing slowly. Easy driving on the freeway, just people going places. I like to check out people in the cars as they go past. Everyone passes me, I'm not in a hurry. Mind in neutral.

Brief look at him, eyes closed, mouth wide open. Not much movement. No movement. No breathing, that I can see. Another brief look, still hasn't moved. No sound coming from the chasm of a mouth. Brief look, but not as brief as last time. The chest is still. Why can't I see it move. Look hard, no ... no movement. Longer look. Feel pulse on arm. Might wake him up and that would be a pity. Don't feel pulse, just feel hand, still warm. Of course it's still warm, it takes ages for dead people to go cold. Long look. Perfectly still, mouth open, eyes closed. Long look at chest, not moving.

What to do now? Very brief looks as I contemplate what to do. I could pull over but nowhere to do it. Could wait for those emergency phones where you can stop. Whoops, just missed one. Realise I'm being silly. He's not dead, just asleep. But maybe he *is* dead. Longer look. No, nothing has changed. What will I do if he is dead? Drive to the end and dial 000. I've got a long way to go before the end of the freeway. What will I do with my life? I'll have to move, but where to? Have to contact his children. I wonder if his ex-wife will come to the funeral. Oh bugger, we never did finish that conversation about whether he wanted to be buried or cremated.

I'll miss him so much. Don't think about that. Brief, loving look. Can't imagine what life will be like without him. I can make a book out of all his poems and stories, including his photos. He'll be famous. Not much fun if he doesn't know. I feel really sad that he's famous but dead. Hang on, he's not dead, just asleep. Brief look. Take deep breath. Need some clarification on the dead situation. Yes, I'll pull over. Nowhere to do it yet. I don't want to be on my own. Tried that, not much fun. Who will I nag? I know that I nag and I know that he doesn't like it. But we joke about it all the time so it can't be that bad. Maybe he just gave up because his life is so terrible. No, it's his bad heart. He told me that he had a dicky ticker. He was only joking. I told him that he can't keep using that excuse to get out of things. What if it was his heart? Now I feel really terrible.

I feel terrible that he died and terrible that I let him. Crestfallen. Brief look. Was that a movement? Yes, that was his hand moving. Brief look. His mouth is closed. Relief. Enormous relief. Head moving, eyes open. He's alive. 'You're alive', I say. He's unmoved by my statement. Back to sleep. Thank goodness I won't have to find a place to pull over. Relaxed, mind in neutral.

Greek Tragedy

Lyn Stewart

T HE MAIN HIGHWAY INTO ATHENS is a six-lane affair, three lanes in each direction with a speed limit of 100 kilometres per hour. We walked along the deep ditch that ran beside it and climbed the embankment so we could cross over to a restaurant on the other side. It was late dusk, still hot, and the sounds of traffic whizzing along the road made it necessary to shout to be heard.

I looked up to see a dark figure flung into the air and fall onto the roadway. 'Oh my God, I hope that was an animal and not a person.' The thud and squeal of brakes seemed to come together. And then the hiss of air-brakes and the sound of wheels, big heavy wheels, going over an obstacle.

It took us a few seconds to reach the roadside. Lying in the middle of the second lane was a man. I heard him groan but he did not move. I looked down the road into the lights of fast on-coming vehicles. One swerved to miss his body and almost met with another vehicle. What could we do? It was too dangerous to run out and reach him. There was a pause in the traffic and I looked across to see two men running towards us from the other side of the highway. Together they picked up the injured man and brought him to our side of the road a couple of metres from us. His face was already swollen and he no longer groaned, his legs lay like snapped twigs. I ran down the embankment to a house and banged on the door. *'Telephono ambulance. Telephono hospidale. Telephono polizia'* I repeated to a woman who stared at my distress. I hoped my broken Italian was international enough, but she didn't comprehend. She didn't go inside to make a call. I returned to the roadside where a few people had arrived. A woman bent over the man and straightened his legs.

People were asking us questions but we couldn't understand Greek. A car pulled up and a young couple ran over. They spoke German but responded to my English. He was a doctor and knelt down over the injured man's body feeling for a pulse. Together they tried to flag down vehicles, but everything going past was too fast to stop. A policeman arrived on his motorbike and began moving us further back from the road. No ambulance came and time went by with nothing happening.

As one of my girlfriends wept I saw a man putting his hand into her bag. 'Sandy, keep your handbag under your arm!' I called.

An empty cattle truck pulled over and the doctor asked for help to put the injured man onto the open tray. He was unconscious but still alive. The doctor jumped aboard and knelt beside him. And that was how it ended; the truck sped away towards Athens and we went back to the camping ground. We never crossed the highway to the restaurant. Somehow we had no appetite for dinner that evening.

A few days later we heard that the man had died soon after reaching the hospital. But no police came to question us. We travelled on to Turkey and three weeks later I returned to Athens and the same camping area. A young man wearing a black armband arrived one afternoon to ask me some questions about what had happened. He was a cousin of the dead man and he hoped to find out if I could describe the vehicle or vehicles involved; information he could make use of. 'Did the police want to ask me questions?' I asked. He thought not.

Water Sports

Chris Dean

T HE CREW OF 'RUBY TUESDAY' shared some remarkable whale experiences while cruising the Whitsunday Islands recently. Complying with exclusion zones around the migrating monsters is always the aim, but when inquisitive humpbacks set you in their sights, *they* call the shots.

Like the day a bunch of hoons came roaring into our peaceful anchorage. Humpbacks. A gang of five.

Our ten-metre catamaran was sitting on a mooring in Manta Ray Bay when a noisy rush of turbulence rounded the Pinnacles, into our cove. Line abreast, they cleared a neighbouring yacht and made a right angle diversion, aimed directly at our beam.

It was amazing and a little unnerving, watching that onslaught of power and energy rolling our way. No graceful manoeuvres here. These guys were out to make their presence felt. They hurtled towards us. Breathing loud and hard. Spumes of water vapour hacking from their blow holes. So close you could almost feel the wet leathery contours of muscle. Individual markings easily distinguishable. One had a white patch covering his left side. Scrapes, gouges and barnacles obvious at this close range. His nearest mate was pockmarked along the back of the head. Cruel adolescent eruptions and craters marring his features. Their leader was as smooth and slick as a Mafia hit man. Were these guys outcasts? Maybe just lads out for a lark, buzzing boats for a bit of fun.

The three on the starboard wing swerved around us at the last moment. One dived underneath. I couldn't see how the fifth got past. I sensed there was no possibility of collision. They knew what they were about.

The group reeled around, pushing through the water in formation, snorting up a cocktail of sea and air that suspended briefly before drifting behind them as a green tinged mist. They hugged the coast and disappeared behind the headland, followed by squeals of delight from the boaties in the next bay.

The whales put on repeat performances in a number of the little coves along that top shore of Hook Island before heading back out to sea. Only then did they slow down, circling and nudging each other. They jumped clear of the water, breaching and fin slapping. Just like some of our local kids, laughing and high-fiving after hooning down the main street of town.

Some weeks we spotted whales every day, but you couldn't count on it. The best encounters snuck up on us.

The catamaran was zipping along under full sail and full sun on the way back from an overnighter at Bait Reef. There wasn't much swell and the teal blue sea had that low winter light sparkle to it when the helmsman sighted two humpbacks breaching. The whales spotted us and detoured our way, tracking alongside for about fifteen minutes. We tried to keep our distance but they were keen for company and followed us. They carried on like a couple of competing street performers trying to outdo each other's high jumps and encouraged by our cheering, upped the tempo. They'd explode out of the water with simultaneous breaches, jumping together before falling apart sideways into gigantic eruptions of whitewater. The show lasted until they tired and rested – backs and humps visible above the water line behind us. Then one rolled sideways and gently lifted his fin to us in farewell.

The mother and baby encounters we had were more

peaceful and moving experiences.

We came across a little one in sheltered water opposite Hamilton Island. It appeared lost and abandoned with no carer in sight – until we spotted a couple of juvenile whales hanging around in the tidal race on the other side of the channel. We guessed Mum had left baby with his older siblings for a while but they were bored with babysitting in the quiet bay and headed over to shoot some waves around the surging water near the reef.

A couple of days later we saw a southbound whale and calf. The calf looked fairly small so I guess it was quite young. It seemed just as curious of us as we were of it. The mother kept a protective position, just below the water line, between her baby and us. But the young'un wanted a closer look. He rolled sideways, exposing his white belly and checked us out with considerable interest. We looked straight into his crinkly little eye. As we passed he raised his pectoral fin and we watched astern as he waved us goodbye.

One flat, hazy winter morning we'd finished snorkelling at Blue Pearl Bay and cleared Hayman Island when one of the crew noticed a water spout ahead. At first it didn't appear spectacular because it was so small that we weren't sure if it was a dolphin or a very young whale. It turned out to be a humpback calf – possibly even a newborn – nudging up to a very still mother drifting on the surface. Through the binoculars we could see that mother wasn't moving and we feared the worst. Until she shifted slightly and sent up an exhausted watery sigh. The young one kept nudging its mother and blowing up little spurts of vapour. Spellbound, we held our breath along with the labouring mum. Slowly, she heaved over onto her back, lifting both pectoral fins skywards as if sending praise to the heavens. The baby floated across her belly. Next the mother gently pivoted, submerging headfirst and poised face down with her tail exposed. There was no sign of the calf. Was it suckling? Another slow roll and the mother whale was floating right way up near the surface again, supporting the baby with her head, while they both rested. This very quiet, calm sequence was one of the many unforgettable experiences of our trip north.

The Yellow Beetle

Hilary Kite

I T WAS SWAZILAND, 1974 and we had a yellow Volkswagen.

Before Gavin and I arrived to work in this tiny landlocked independent African Kingdom, we were told a car would be supplied for our use. And there she was – a small, quite elderly, bright yellow Volkswagen Beetle. We fell instantly in love with her and, although our sojourn there was short, we travelled many adventurous miles together through the often rugged, sometimes dangerous, but always uniquely beautiful African countryside.

Our Beetle did a great job and faithfully carried us far and wide in all sorts of conditions, the roads being mainly unsealed and in varying states of repair.

The car did break down on numerous occasions. Luckily, it was in the main Manzini shopping street when she refused to budge one day. A very helpful gentleman spent some considerable time fiddling under the bonnet – or whatever you call the cover of an engine at the back of a car. He finally asked me to try to start it and it leapt into life. I was so overjoyed I too leapt – out of the car – to thank him. I learnt a lesson that day – don't take your foot off the accelerator and let the engine die when someone has just managed to get it started.

Then there was the time we took a trip to a game park. The car was having starting problems and every night we had to find a slope to park on so that we could more easily push-start her the next morning. Unfortunately, we were not on a slope when the car stalled on a game drive one afternoon, and even more unfortunate was the fact that one very large lone bull elephant came lumbering out of the bush straight towards us. I had been told that a lone bull elephant was often aggressive. I had also been told that when an elephant flaps his ears it means trouble. There was no mistaking the enormous flapping ears. We were sitting right in his path with no chance of getting away and a little yellow car would afford us no protection at all if he turned nasty. We sat and waiting for the crunch which luckily did not come, the giant creature deciding at the last moment to veer off to the side. It was some time before I felt brave enough to pop out and push until the car spluttered into life.

Another irksome trait of this car was her propensity for the keys to stay in the ignition when the door was closed and locked. This mostly seemed to happen when I was out shopping and I became quite skilled in lifting the latch with a bent wire coat hanger which Val Smith in the Ladies Dress Shop was happy to lend me - although, after returning a number of misshapen hangers, I suspect she kept one under the counter especially for me.

One particularly memorable weekend, our friends Alan and Marion came to stay. They were not small people and we had to drive up to the little mining town of Pigg's Peak on a very windy gravel road with a precipitous drop-off on one side. Fitting us all in the Beetle was the first challenge. It was a real-life enactment of the elephant joke: 'How do you fit four elephants into a Mini?' We girls of course had to do the undignified scrambling into the back seat and the even more undignified bottoms-first erupting out again. Gavin was never one to let less than optimum conditions affect the speed he thought was appropriate - and this was always as fast as the car would go. His driving skills were put to the test that day with hair-raising moments, nearly skidding off the road and dodging stray goats and cows in the misty dark on the way back.

But even Gavin was not up to ramming antelope on a lonely African road in a small car, which did not have even a hardy engine in front for some protection. However, his boss, the Reverend Zephaniah Kunene, who was his passenger that night, was only thinking of a nice meal of roast venison when a Steenbok appeared in the road in front of them, dazzled by the car's lights. 'HIT IT, HIT IT!' was the frantic cry. Fortunately, sanity prevailed and the buck was able to leap safely off into the veld. Its happy escape did nothing for Gavin, who had to endure the wrath of one irate Swazi gentleman who felt cheated of a good dinner.

One of the last outings of our stay in Swaziland was to attend the Independence Day Celebrations. We had just parked our trusty VW at the stadium when two buses pulled up. In a bright and noisy bustle of colour, out poured the King's sixty wives, decked in traditional finery, to take part in the ceremony. In 1974, old King Sobhuza II was still on the throne and, by the time he died, was reported to have at least seventy wives and a thousand grandchildren.

The present King Mswati III has, to date, only fourteen wives, but custom demands that he marry a woman from every clan, so further marriages are on the cards. From all reports, this will not prove too onerous a tradition for him to follow. And the wives – well, they no longer travel in buses, but each drives her own German-made car but not, I suspect, a yellow Volkswagen Beetle.

Thursday Afternoons

Steve Jacobson

Discarded in haste,

clothes lie scattered on the floor.

Curtains billow at the open window

below in the street, traffic noise.

Flesh against flesh, the lovers re-awake -

lust has cooled with the heat of the day,

their passion faded with the afternoon light.

It's time to dress, time to go.

Sheets are smoothed, the bed is straightened.

The gently closing door echoes the parting kiss -

unspoken is the promise of next Thursday

Hot Stuff

Liz May

'Go! Sun, sun, sun, sun...oooooooooooo.' This song by The Sunrays jolts me back to my childhood - sea, sand and surf - integral components of an Aussie upbringing, even if you lived miles from the beach in the outer western suburbs.

For most ordinary, Australian kids, trips to the beach are an essential feature of summer life. In the 1950s, there were bubble swimming costumes, plastic talisman sandals, melting tar that scalded the soles of your feet as you painfully danced across the road, hoping to be the first one to plunge into the rolling surf. A trip to the beach was a major excursion as all the paraphernalia was gathered together and stuffed into the overloaded car - spades, buckets, towels, swimmers, boards (the multi coloured polystyrene kick board or if you were lucky a rubber, surf plane!), picnic lunch, zinc cream and the ubiquitous beach umbrella which launched itself skywards at the merest puff of breeze. Everyone would cram into the car, which would eventually grind to a halt in the traffic as it banked up on the single lane Mona Vale Road. Here you would sit impatiently, dripping with perspiration, sticking to the vinyl upholstery, with windows wound right down in your un-air-conditioned car.

Balmoral and Collaroy were two of our favourite family destinations. The sight of The Michelin Tyre Man was enough to send us into paroxysms, as this was the landmark that heralded the proximity of the ocean. My father would then break into his habitual joke. 'Can you see the sea plane? I can see the sea plain.'

At day's end there would be togs with the crutch full of sand, a pink body, rapidly darkening into red, with criss-crossing where the straps had been and later on a peeling nose and a thousand more freckles.

As a teenager a trip to the beach with your friends was not merely a social outing, but an opportunity, 'to work on your tan'. This was best achieved by spending an entire day in the blazing sun, basting your body with Johnson's baby oil, interspersed with brief dips in the water not only to cool off, but more importantly to acquire a salt encrusted layer that would hasten the frying process. It was like rubbing salt and oil into the pork in order to achieve the crispiest crackling! A tan was our Holy Grail and we suffered endlessly in its pursuit. Our family remedy for a lobster red skin was to immerse it in very hot water' to take the sting out' my mother intoned, but it merely numbed the area, or perhaps the brain.

By this stage, the bubble swimming costume had been transformed into a little-boy-leg two-piece, which finally morphed into an itsy-bitsy teeny-weeny bikini, as we gained in confidence and wore down the objections of our parents to such scanty attire. However, this did mean that we were exposing more skin to intense UV rays, thus creating the potential for an almost all over tan - the darker the better. You could never feel that you had been on holidays unless you returned to school or uni sporting a deep, rich tan.

In addition to a tan it was also de rigeur to have bleached, blond hair. As artificially dyeing your hair was banned at our school, we developed other techniques to circumvent the rules. Lemon juice applied to the hair while wet and then set, by sitting in the sun, ensured subtle highlights. You just had to make certain that you washed out all the pips. For a more enduring effect I chose Bon Ami, although I'm told Ajax worked just as well, to give a bleached, beachy effect. Of course your hairstyle had to conform as well; if curly then it had to be ironed straight and if short, to achieve the Cilla Black long kiss-curl look, you applied sticky tape to the curls, which you wound closely and attached to the side of your face. In the morning you had an instant dermabrasion as well.

Trannies in the 1960s were transistor radios and they went everywhere with us including to the beach, where they invariably filled up with sand, eventually clogging their works and hastening their demise. That is, unless you did as I did, and acquired a boy friend expert in the restoration of radios. The Good Guys on 2SM provided us with the music to tan by—the Beach Boys tantalized us with scenes of exotic California beaches, the Delltones, encouraged us 'to hang five' or Little Pattie, who had us stomping at Maroubra.

Oh how I longed to be cool like Sandra Dee or Sally Field in the guise of Gidget, a cool, popular teenager with perfectly flicked hair, neat, tanned figure and a Moondoggie boyfriend. But after all those years of striving for the perfect tan all I have left are freckles, dry skin and skin cancers!

They Say I Have Dementia

Judy Farley

I HEAR THEM TALKING when they think I'm asleep. I suppose they're right. That would explain why this cotton wool feeling in my head never seems to disappear. Why can I recollect playing with my brothers and sisters and can't remember what I had for breakfast? It seems like yesterday we waded through the river on the way home from school to find Mum still kneeling on the river bank; there were seven of us and the washing pile never ended.

When I was a young man, tall and strong, I wanted to stay that way forever. As a soldier fighting in the steamy jungles of Borneo and New Guinea, I thought I was invincible. I am still tall but now I have no strength, my muscles wasted from recent inactivity. I didn't expect my life to end like this.

Here I lie in a hospital bed. I feel like a baby, being fed and watered and changed every little while. I wish I could have stayed at home. I knew my own house, even though I kept getting lost. Sometimes this little voice in my head tells me to do something odd. The nights are the worst. I'm afraid I'll fall out of this strange narrow high bed. Sometimes the nurse puts my mattress on the floor and then I feel more secure.

I have trouble remembering names. I think my wife is Mary. Maybe this isn't right because when I say that she laughs and says "I'm not Mary" and she calls herself something else. Even though she keeps reminding me, I still can't find her real name. It is the same with all the people I care about the most; the names just aren't there.

There are familiar people who come and see me, like my doctor and my brothers and sisters. There's another doctor who sees me and she has the kindest eyes. Yesterday my old neighbour Harry visited and I remembered his name. He had a tear in his eye as he shook my hand.

My minister calls and sees me daily. She always says a prayer for me. Sometimes I just close my eyes and listen, sometimes I smile at her. I love to hear her gentle voice.

Last week I saw my only great grandson. He won't remember me, but I will always have the image of him toddling around my room on unsteady legs. I watched his every move, storing the precious memory.

All these loved ones around me. I have so much to be thankful for.

Now I can rest.

Love, Dad

Liz May

T HEY CRUNCH THEIR WAY up the red gravel drive to the boarding school. He tightens his grip on his mother's soft, gloved hand. Forty years on he can still see the sterile entrance hall leading into the Reception Room, with a Grand Piano anchored in the centre. The room smells of beeswax and the dust motes dance in the afternoon light. He has always been fascinated by light, and wonders where the dust goes when the light is absent.

He is six years old and his father is far away fighting the Japanese on some island whose name he can't pronounce, but he can show you its location on a map. His mother shows him the postcards his father sends with exotic looking people on the front, smiling broadly, but with little covering their dark bodies. He feels uncomfortable with their nakedness. Their black Nugget hair is wiry like the steel wool his mother uses to scrub the battered old saucepans. Most of the blue smudged lines scribbled on the back of the cards are indecipherable. But there are two words he always recognises – 'Love, Dad.'

Who *is* Dad? He can't picture this man, but he subconsciously associates him with the aroma of Amphora tobacco, which still clings to the pipes on the stand on the old upright piano in their lounge room. Dark brown, with a gentle curve, the tips of the pipe stems are covered in white streaks left from his father's yellowed teeth. The boy loves to climb on the rungs of the piano stool to the cracked leather seat, obsessed with scratching off the peeling turquoise paint from its metal studs. Perched high, he stretches and is just able to grasp hold of a pipe. He drinks in its sweet smell and sucks the end until it becomes wet and dribbly, before carefully returning it to its rightful position.

The Wedding Terrorists

Irene Waters

O UR FRIEND JACK'S DAUGHTER was getting married. As
usual, a limit to the number of guests was the order of
the day and we were not that close that we warranted an
invitation. We were close enough to be asked if we would
volunteer our assistance on the day - me to serve drinks and
Roger to assist in the kitchen with the pre-wedding hors
d'oeuvres. This would give us the opportunity to admire the
bride whilst using our skills as past restaurateurs. We readily
agreed.

We arrived at the venue by the river an hour before the
ceremony. Already the guests had started mingling. There was
total chaos in the kitchen. Jack's sister, Janet, was a caterer and
had taken on the task of providing the food, preparing the
finger food for prenuptial nibbles, preparing the salads to go
with the barbecue and the preparation of dessert. The groom
was in charge of the barbecue.

It was obvious that I was more needed in the kitchen than I was serving drinks. The guests were quite happy helping themselves - liberally. I set to preparing smoked oysters on little toasts and finger breads. Roger busied himself at the ovens in the attempt to get the pastries and other hot treats ready. This was difficult to say the least as two of the ovens were not functioning leaving a very small oven and a microwave. We had worked in worse circumstances and were unfazed.

The huge barbecue was being looked after by the groom and the best men. They were all chefs and all wanted to be chiefs. Roger tried in vain to get them to turn over the cooking to him. In frustration he told me, 'They are cooking it far too hot. I've turned it down several times and they keep turning it up again. I give up. I'm going to leave it to them.' I made the appropriate clucking noises and off he stormed.

Suddenly the din of people talking and laughing ceased. At last we could hear the musicians strumming their chords. Everyone had disappeared to the river bank some 400 yards down the hill for the ceremony. No-one had said a word to us. Janet had left no instructions as to what she wanted done with the salads. I decided that the best thing for me to do was to clean the kitchen and wash up. Roger would do whatever preparation he felt necessary.

The peace was broken when one of the band members came racing in, visibly disturbed. 'The BBQ's on fire!' he screamed and ran out. We followed arriving just in time to witness the massive bang as the glass lid imploded covering the meat with glass. We turned off the gas and put the fire out before looking at each other. 'What the hell do we do now?' we both thought. 'Carry the meat into the kitchen and we'll scrub it and see what the damage is,' Roger commanded.

Trip after trip we made to the BBQ. There was every joint of meat imaginable. There was deer hunted that week by the groom, supposed road-kill kangaroo run down by the groom on the way to the wedding and more conventional pork, beef and sides of lamb. It had been jam-packed onto the BBQ and, with the incredibly high heat they had been using and with the fat dripping down from meat on top, the outsides of the beasts were black whilst the insides were raw and, in the case of the deer, jellified blubber.

On arrival in the kitchen we threw it in a sink, ran running water over it and transferred it piece by piece to the other sink. The force of the implosion had buried square pieces of safety glass well inside the joints. We scrubbed the outside, removing most of the glass and other pieces we picked out by hand. We then made two piles. One was meat we considered still suspect that needed going over with a fine tooth comb. The other was meat which we thought was probably okay.

As we were carrying out this procedure, the ceremony must have concluded as Janet arrived back in the kitchen. She stood in the kitchen door, a horrified expression on her face. 'What the hell are you two doing?' she screamed. As we explained the situation her face fell. 'What should I do? What am I going to feed all these people?'

'The call is yours, Janet, but I think this meat is glass-free and we could finish it off in the oven,' Roger suggested.

Her face worked as she thought through the ramifications of a guest eating some glass and what she would do if she had nothing to feed them. 'We'll do it!' For the first time that day we worked harmoniously together, all united in the single purpose of feeding the masses.

We decided that we would carve the meat and serve it from the kitchen rather than put it out for the guests to carve for themselves which had been the original plan. That way we could vet every bit of meat as it was served. The salads still went out on the tables. The meat did not look at all attractive and people baulked at the jellified venison and the dark meat of the kangaroo steaks. Nobody knew what anything was, including us. It reached a point that when asked 'what is that meat?' I would reply with 'what do you want it to be?'

At the conclusion of the serving and the cleaning up, we were told that we could have a meal and that we could take the left-over meat home for the dogs. We declined both offers but accepted a drink with Janet. We had a good laugh about our evening. She told us the full extent of her horror when she had walked through the door and seen us scrubbing the meat. 'I thought,' she said, 'Who are these people? Where had Jack got them from? I was convinced you were a couple of wedding terrorists.'

Fate of the Plate

Sue Urby

Few do choose to scan a plate

and think upon its size,

then ponder whether square or round

is pleasing to the eyes.

Some then consider whence it came,

from English or Chinese,

perhaps it could be Prussian

or even Japanese.

Some books do state, the plate began

a simple wooden vessel.

I wonder then how it was balanced -

by knee or on a trestle.

It's said, at least eight centuries past,

came pewter on the scene,

afforded just by noblemen –

for others just a dream.

Much later still, refined again,

came porcelain for the masses,

and at a price all could afford,

accessible to all classes.

Knees Up

Sue Urby

BACK THEN, IT WAS YOUR KNEES OR NOTHING on which to rest your dinner plate. The improvement to this came with the idea of the 'board', namely the plain board. It was hung on the wall when not in use. At mealtimes, this single board rested across the diners' laps. Well, not for your high and mighty, that is, but for the poor of the Middles Ages. Tough times they were. Diners, different shapes and sizes, would sit the length of the board. Maybe this is where the balancing act originated, all concentrating while passing the HP or the Tomato Sauce.

If having more people for dinner than would sit around your board, I imagine you'd resort to calling over the fence to your neighbour. It would go something like:

'Hello Fred. Art thou there?'

'Aye, Tom, what canst I do for thee?'

'Couldst thou lend me thy plain board this night, we're having a bit of a do, d'ye see. I'd be ever so much obliged.'

'Aye, Tom, I canst do that for thee, we'll use our knees tonight. Keep the noise down, will ye man? I've to be up early in the morn.'

No point in asking: 'Canst I please leave the board?' There could be another three still eating. Worse still if a child had to sit there until he'd eaten all his greens. Mum would soon learn not to ask if anyone would like seconds; there'd be no takers offering to fetch the salt; you'd push your plate away only the once and no need to mention: 'Elbows off the board.'

Round-table discussions would not have happened, but maybe board meetings? The saying 'Up 123' definitely had to have come from this era.

A Writing Group would've had great difficulty meeting along the board, balancing their work, tea and passing cake around.

How grateful; I feel sitting at my table.

Hope You Like It

Irene Waters

THINGS HAD TO CHANGE AND IMMEDIATELY. On arrival at our new venture - White Grass Resort, Tanna, Vanuatu - my husband, Roger, and I found the equipment in the kitchen was minimal. A gas powered bar fridge and a two burner Primus was the sum total. Not only was the equipment lacking, the provisions were non-existent. We had to be able to provide a reasonable menu and until we had electricity we were going to have to do it with what was there already.

Because a beast was slaughtered only once a week at the back of the general store this made providing meat difficult. The meat varied from the 'best melt in your mouth steak you'd ever had' to the toughest. We discovered that its tenderness depended on how stressed the animal had been in the lead up to its death. We sent our cook in on killing day to determine what this was likely to be before purchase. He didn't buy much meat if he thought it was going to be tough.

Our menu therefore revolved mainly around seafood and chicken. Roger and Peter, the cook, would go to the market held under the Banyan tree in Lenakel and wander around looking at the produce the women sitting on their mats in the dirt were selling. Everyone was of course offering exactly the same thing. We had forgotten with Woolworths that fruit and vegetables are seasonal. Everyone was asking the same price as well - a society devoid of competition. Roger and Peter would come home from market with umpteen live chickens, crabs with a tether rope tied to one leg, occasionally slipper lobsters and a lot of fruit and vegetables.

So that we could keep as many cold drinks in the bar fridge as possible all the animals were kept alive until needed. To get over the difficulties associated with this we asked our guests to order their evening meal at lunchtime. This was done by saying 'we don't know what time you will get back from the volcano tour and as people are usually hungry when they return, it's good not to have to wait for your meal.' Everyone happily complied. Off they would go on tour and we would spend the afternoon chasing chickens, sending the lobster catcher to the rocks or fisherman out to sea in order to provide whatever they had ordered. Most of our guests had no idea.

One non-touring guest watched Joseph, cleaver in hand, chasing a chicken round the restaurant. On another occasion the only chicken we had left had flown up a tree. Even the nimble coconut climbing gardening boys could not catch it. We had to apologise to our guest on his return. We told him, 'Your dinner has gone up a tree! Would you mind choosing something else?'

Desserts were missing from our menu. Fruit salad was easily added but we felt we needed more than that. Roger had the brainwave of pancakes with lemon. That night the resort was full. In addition a government dinner had swelled the restaurant numbers to around forty. It was a real struggle cooking for that number with the cooker Peter had. The flame was yellow instead of blue and gave off very little heat. The first order for a pancake came and Roger went to work. After half an hour I went into the kitchen to see what was going on. I don't know how many attempts he had made but he was in a severely stressed state. They were either, cooking to be like rubber, breaking up into little islands or sticking to the pan. Eventually there was one that Roger reluctantly sent out. We weren't surprised that we didn't get any compliments. As a result we donated to the restaurant our four burner cooker with oven that we had been given as a wedding present. We couldn't watch Peter trying to cook on his antiquated model any longer. Peter spent the next morning working on the pancake recipe. He finally perfected a way of cooking them that suited our conditions of powdered milk and Chinese flour. From that day they were sold as Peter's Pancakes and became famous as far afield as Vila.

After several months we got our electrical system up and running. We could then pre-cook the curries and 'spag bols' which made life much easier for us. This caused us much amusement. The freezer was in our house which was approximately 300 yards from the restaurant. Between the resort and our house was pitch black nothingness. An order would come in and one of us would grab the torch and run to the house. Everything would be pulled out of the chest freezer in an attempt to find the desired article. Once found, we would then run back to the restaurant where the reheating process would take place. Our labelling system left a bit to be desired and often the wrong item would be brought back. So we were off running again. We all took turns and we were all jolly fit as a result.

One day a lunch guest asked me what I would recommend he should order '... the chicken curry or the chicken soy?' I recommended the curry. I placed the order and off Joseph ran. He came back empty handed not having been able to find any curries. Off to the house Roger went. I went back in to the restaurant and said to the guest, 'I've been thinking about it. You really should try the chicken soy as you can get curries anywhere. Chicken soy really is an island delicacy.' He agreed and I went back to the kitchen to tell Peter that when Roger came back with the chicken soy our guest would happily have it. Roger came back with the soy. Peter started to cook it only to discover that it was in reality a chicken curry. At this point Roger said he would go and talk to our guest and persuade him to have the chicken curry. Our guest pointed out that 'Irene says I really should try the chicken soy'. At that point Roger told him the truth and he agreed to have the curry. Roger returned to the kitchen where Peter happily told him, 'emia awight. Me fella convertum curry. Emia numbwan soy.' I carried the meal out to the table and said, 'I don't know what it is now but I hope you enjoy it.'

Dinner in Delhi

Hilary Kite

'Would you prefer chicken or fish for dinner?' asks Shilpa, the social worker, as we get off the bus. She has invited me to stay the night at her home and we have travelled together from the Delhi slum where we work at the Community Health Centre.

I wonder about eating fish in Delhi, so far from the sea. And knowing that the Yamuna River, which we cross every morning on our way to work, is the dirtiest river in India, gives me no confidence in anything caught in those muddy, polluted waters. I plumb for chicken.

I had noticed the piles of small cages of live chickens at street stalls and optimistically thought that they supplied the eggs sold from large trays. But I had also noticed that in the afternoons the number of chickens appeared fewer than in the mornings.

I do not have long to wonder at this because we soon

stop at one of these open air street markets and a nice-looking chook is selected. This is dispatched with the least amount of fuss. Just a rickety table top, tilted to allow blood to drain off into the open drain running at our feet, a sharp knife and a young boy with a leafy branch to wave away the flies. I concentrate for a while on watching the live fish swimming around the plastic buckets in the next stall and ten minutes later we walk off with skinned chicken pieces, the makings of a chicken curry.

Shilpa's home turns out to be a room on the roof of a block of flats. It is a pukka building – permanent brick as opposed to a mud, and may be added onto at any time when the owner finds a few extra funds. The room is just big enough for a bed, a TV, a cupboard and table. Shilpa has to go outside to her kitchen, a tiny room with a bench and hotplate and a top shelf for ingredients. The doors of both rooms are metal with large locks.

The bathroom, shared with a young couple who live on the other side of the roof, is square and windowless, with a tap on one wall and a drain hole in the floor. An immersion heater in a bucket provides hot water but, on my visit, the weather is steamy and a cool bath is welcome.

And the toilet? This is a squat, right at the corner of the roof with waist-high walls and no roof. It must be interesting during the monsoon season. It too is shared by the young couple, so I decide singing may be a good idea.

While we watch a snowy episode of an American sitcom in Hindi, Shilpa kneads dough for the chapattis. I try to help with the rolling out, but would never make a good Indian wife. It was in the movie 'Bend it Like Beckham', when the Punjabi mother of the soccer-playing teenager despairs that her daughter 'can't even make a round chapatti!'

After dinner Shilpa shows me her treasures – special silk saris and photos kept in a suitcase under her bed. She tells of her daughter who lives with her parents and whom she sees twice a year. Her husband walked out on her when the baby didn't turn out to be the eagerly anticipated son. For her, this is a shameful secret and she entreats me not to tell anyone at the Centre. As she talks, I contemplate the gaudy statue of the elephant god, Ganesh, in his niche in the wall, bedecked with a dusty garland of marigolds. I find myself praying that he might live up to his reputation and grant Shilpa success and a happy life.

And as we sleep – me on her bed, and her on the floor

beside me, lulled by the drone of a million mosquitoes, I know that I am very far away from home.

A Weight on my Mind

Liz May

'Oh that this too, too solid flesh would melt…' In Shakespeare's play *Hamlet* his main character, Hamlet, in one of his interminable soliloquies reflects on his statuesque physique. Well, I know just what he means. You have probably heard of a Post-Modern interpretation of literature, now here is another reading of literature called the Neo-Adiposal. This allows the reader to deconstruct the text from a physical point of view. A close reading of the play from this perspective reveals that Hamlet bears all the hallmarks of a person who is weight challenged. Just like me!

Hamlet suffers from inactivity to the point of psychological paralysis. In the mould of a number of obese individuals he is unable to grasp the nettle and face his problems. He is rendered incapable by procrastination, or is it that procrastination renders him incapable? Anyone who is about to embark on a restricted dietary regime can identify with his position, assuring themselves that they are incapable of adopting any measures for change because:

'Today is too hot.'

'Today is too cold.'

'There's a celebration this week involving eating copious amounts of sweet and fattening substances so it is futile to begin now.'

'It would be preferable to wait until the beginning of the week, month, year or even millennium.' As Shakespeare put it, 'Tomorrow and tomorrow and tomorrow...' Wrong play ... I know.

Just as Hamlet took out his frustrations on Ophelia most would-be-dieters prefer to project their inadequacies on to others. This means that society is to blame because the social conventions are positively skewed to favour the lean with beautiful as its collocation. For the obese, another group of pariahs are the metabolically blessed, the members of which can eat exactly what they like and never put on any weight. A fact that is largely unobserved is that this group rarely consumes high calorie foods and if they do so it is never surreptitiously being always in the public domain. Thus, as a result of their paranoia the weight-challenged indulge in the popular pursuit of ancestor bashing. This means that one's ancestors can be held entirely accountable for the dieter's inability to remove unwanted kilos. Partaking in this particular pastime sees me admonishing my grandmother as the source of all my excess baggage. 'Look at my grandmother,' I say, 'How can I possibly have a chance in the battle of the bulge with genes like those? Indeed it's my entire Celtic ancestry at fault. Just think about how many miles of material is required to fashion a kilt. It's all down to my Scottish forebears, who sported such ample girths!'

Many dieters seek advice in order to tackle their addictions and much of the wisdom that is imparted by their mentors is as useful as the advice tendered to Hamlet by Polonius such as, 'Neither a lender nor a borrower be...' Over the past forty-eight years I have been offered similar tenets. When I was twelve years old and in Year Seven, one of my classmates advised me that Vita Weets spread liberally with butter and Vegemite were substantial fare for an adolescent, as well as a nutritionally well-balanced meal, particularly if the butter was sufficient to ooze through the myriad holes in the biscuits. Thus began a lifetime of dieting based on sound dietary principles.

There have, of course, been other advisors of far greater

repute and authority who have been of invaluable assistance in my life long struggle. Weight Watchers, a modicum of success here, but I have watched religiously as my weight has steadily climbed... Easy Slim - now there is an example of an oxymoron. Jenny Craig - Magda's success has been inspirational, but I don't think I can contemplate the synthetic concoctions anymore. The CSIRO Diet - not for the vegetarian, puts a hole in your budget as well. Atkins Diet - well he did die of cancer didn't he? The Choose to Lose programme run by a well-respected hospital - I chose to lose, but unfortunately my body did not. The ultimate diet for the chocoholic was the one that espoused the philosophy that you need to challenge your body with the foods you love, eating as much as you want over a few days and thus lessening your cravings. Unfortunately I lost track of the time. This antipasto dish of diets has been successful in depleting me of some of my assets, but they were mostly of a monetary nature!

So the quest continues. 'The spirit is willing, but the flesh...'

Hard Grind

Steve Jacobson

I FEEL SORRY FOR MY DENTIST because I know that no-one actually **enjoys** visiting him. People **must**, sooner or later - probably later for some when it should have been sooner. But his patients don't visit because he's such a lovely bloke; they only go under sufferance because it's for the best: relieving pain, prolonging the useful life of one's teeth or cosmetic enhancement.

Given my history with dentists, it's surprising that I still go at all. My teeth aren't wonderful but at least they're mine and I aim to keep them that way if I can. When I first visited my current dentist (and he is a lovely bloke) he inspected my mouth and commented, 'Hmm, looks like you're not going to be a stranger to my surgery for a few years yet!' I'm not sure whether he meant that my teeth would last a bit longer, ensuring further business, or whether a lot needed fixing. I didn't like to ask.

As a small child in WWII England, there wasn't much money to spare, but mother was always conscientious about taking us to the family dentist. This involved the excitement of a train trip to the nearest big town and the prospect of a teashop treat afterwards 'if we were good'. The treat always included sticky buns and soft drinks, so the visits weren't all bad from our point of view, if not particularly beneficial to our teeth.

When I was about 9, my pharmacist father bought a chemist's shop with house attached in a small village. The shop itself was newly-built, but the adjoining house behind was wonderfully old and interesting: the best part was an attic that my sister and I used as our private hidey-hole. The downside to our new accommodation was concealed behind a locked door leading back to a small ground-floor room. To our horror we found this room was permanently set up as a dentist's surgery, complete with gruesome-looking, antique dental equipment which I sometimes see these days in museums.

'She's a very nice lady,' said mother, planting seeds of consolation for what were to be apparently regular visits. Our parents must have thought this was all very convenient, having a dentist on the premises, and not only for the rent. I still remember the 'nice lady' distinctly. She was short, elderly and grumpy, her name was Miss Wilkins and she visited every Thursday, without fail. Fortunately my sister and I were then sent away to boarding school, so we didn't have to live with the Thursday routine: the stream of locals trooping into the surgery and the incessant whine of Miss Wilkins' drill which could be mistaken for Council workers digging up the road. But on the first Thursday of each school holiday we knew it was our turn for the regular check-up that nearly always meant something painful was about to happen.

My sister and I devised a plan. Immediately after breakfast on that first Thursday, we would disappear up to our attic for the morning. At some stage, we knew mother would come to the bottom of the stairs and call out 'Miss Wilkins can see you now, come down now, please!' We pretended not to hear and, quickly and quietly, climbed out through the attic window onto the roof, hiding in the space between the old and new buildings. Mother would call again impatiently and, getting no reply, would come up into the attic to find us. Naturally, she knew where we were, and we knew that she knew. But she was too big to climb out after us, so all she could do was to stand at the open window and say, 'Come back in here at once, I know you're out there, you're very naughty girls!'

We had to come down eventually and face the dreaded dragon-lady in her lair. No pain-killing injections or soft words were used to ease the discomfort. The drilling seemed to go on for ages and ages and the whole experience was medieval torture: we squirmed in the chair protesting as best we could against the poking and prodding of metal instruments into and between the teeth, the loud grinding of the drill, Miss Wilkins' bad breath and, of course, the pain. We survived.

Behind the house there was a garden planted with beautiful old roses. As we helped mother to dig over the ground now and then, we often found the odd molar or incisor buried under the roses. We guessed that Miss Wilkins had been asked to throw the by-products of her handiwork onto the garden – blood and bone is good for roses, isn't it?

As I said, my teeth aren't wonderful but they are my own and I am grateful to mother for being educated to look after them. And sometimes, when my husband and I join the caravanning grey nomads and I find myself in the ablutions block with other ladies of a similar age, I feel a bit smug to notice that I'm about the only one there who can still clean her teeth without taking them out.

Panic

Margaret Collett

A ND I'M EARLY I KNEW I'D BE TOO EARLY. It means I have to sit here and listen to the noises from behind that door I've been given a form to fill in how can a person be expected to think neatly at a time like this, for heaven's sake and that girl behind the desk I know she knows I'm scared even before I put these ticks at the bottom of the page she can hardly suppress a smile surely she won't be the one assisting him no that'll be another perfectly groomed porcelain skinned twenty something well since they're going to ask yes I have an unusually strong fear of dentists and no bloody wonder and I bet this one will be no different despite what people say this is a pretty boring waiting room what can I concentrate on look at that wood panelling is it 70s or 80s who cares why doesn't he come out of his lair and get me it's not as if he should be running late it's only nine am for Pete's sake I can hear voices from that room maybe they've heard about me there's two men talking maybe he knows he'll need help to hold me down what an awful string sculpture when were they around? I hope his instruments are a bit more modern I've brought a copy of Silas Marner with me because it fits into my bag but not really waiting room material I know if I get up and look at those magazines near the door I'll be out never to return they look pretty daggy anyway what I suspect to be the surgery door's opening and two men are coming out just as I thought one of them's pushing eighty and he's going straight to Miss Perfect Teeth behind the counter must be the patient well he survived the other one did seem nice although I find it's best not to make eye contact no I don't mind waiting a few minutes wow he is nice but he might be the assistant I'll wait all day and just get checked out by a kind of vicarious dentistry by sitting here in this very brown room I hope my breath doesn't smell it shouldn't I cleaned my teeth about five times, flossed, Listerined, flossed, and then had about four hot mints on the way here my hair looks really daggy today I know he's going to see how bad my skin is all those acne scars and now hairs on my top lip and I wish I was beautiful oh God, the door's open again and yes I'm Marg and no I don't mind following him who ever heard of a dentist shaking hands I don't think I'll let go and then we'll be caught in a very pleasant position for the rest of the day but no the assistant another even younger version of her outside has started that swilling thing and here's my bib I'll be needing this just relax are you kidding there's really nothing solid to hold onto with this chair not impressed he's taken my glasses too which might help in some silly way to blur the pain and he's put a mask and glasses on probably can't bear to look at me and I'm sure my breath smells he's so gentle even his voice I think I could love this man in another life the print on the ceiling is one of those Heidelberg school ones Roberts or McCubbin no it's no use I have to close my eyes why doesn't he offer me an injection gas anything that sucker thing has started I know I'm going to dribble all over the place won't be able to go shopping have to go straight home what made me think I could go shopping anyway he's picked up something I'm not going to look I know it'll be sharp that strangled kitten noise has started and I can feel him moving above me in another life he would bend and kiss me gently that's not going to happen here. I hate this man I love this man.

The Catch

Lyn Stewart

He knew this was the moment -

all that had gone before led to this.

Follow the ball, grab at the cap and fling the damn thing away.

Eyes calculating the trajectory, knees bent, half turn, seven or
eight strides -
no, a couple of shorter ones, then up.

Stretch that arm, fingers out -

the ones Grandma thought should play the piano .

I had watched that loose-limbed lad back his way to the
outfield -
knees bent he planted himself in waiting.

Now chance arrives - he sweeps off his cap as a courtier to his
queen.
Head skyward, eyes fixed on the prize -

prancing sideways then backwards like a two-stepper without a
partner.

Then that balletic leap.

Stretching up, fingers ready to cup the red bird inexorably
drawn to the nest,
balancing arm pushing down with fingers splayed across an
octave.
The crowd rises to its feet, flags saluting the magnificent
moment -
the winning catch.

The Leper

Irene Waters

I FITTED INTO MY FAMILY in the same way I fitted into society. I didn't. My father was a minister and my mother one of the original Quiz Kids. My 'outside world' expected me to be either a goody two shoes or a younger example of my mother and brilliant elder brother. I was neither of these things. I was an exuberant, easily bored child who looked forward to school just to have company, to skip rope or play hopscotch. We lived at the end of town where the church and grounds occupied the entire block. The church was on a fairly busy road (in a small country town this doesn't mean a lot), but our house was at the rear of the church and bordered by parkland and the river on two sides. There were no children nearby with whom to play except the Catholic children who lived opposite the church, but they had been deemed unsuitable companions.

I had learnt that the friends of my choice were not to be

brought home. When I was five I took Raymond Fardon home. He had asked me to marry him and as I was giving this serious consideration, I felt I should take him home to meet my parents. That was a real disaster as he was given short shrift and sent home promptly, never to darken our door again. He then totally ignored me and took up with another girl whose parents were no doubt more accommodating.

My next failure was when the Tattersall girl came to town. Her father owned Tattersall's Hotels all down the eastern seaboard. They would spend three to six months in each town overseeing the local hotel operation. I immediately clicked with Rhonda. We were inseparable at school and walked home together as the hotel was on my route. I stayed at the hotel with her a little too long one afternoon and was forbidden to go there again. When I attempted to bring her to our house my mother always had an alternative arrangement and Rhonda left town before an appropriate time could be found.

My mother turned yellow one day and the doctor diagnosed her as contagious. My brother and I were banned from attending school so we wouldn't pass on this dreadful disease. My brother's spirits soared as he could continue reading the book he'd started and then start another and another. My heart sank. No-one to play with. How was I going to cope? It would be the same as our Christmas holidays at the beach where the other members of my family would lie in bed all morning reading their books and eating their chocolates whilst I annoyed them all, agitating to go to the beach. Even threatening to hang myself moved no-one from their books except my brother. He stirred out of bed as he wanted to watch. It only gave him something to crow about when I failed in my attempt. I had tied a slip knot in my noose.

How was I going to survive this enforced isolation? Then it came to me. My father had given a children's address in church about the leper and Jesus. I could be the leper! I raced up to the church and hid behind one of the fir trees. Whenever anyone approached I would jump out from behind the tree yelling and waving my arms around wildly 'Stay away! I'm unclean! I'm a leper and my mother is yellow. Beware! Don't come near me or you'll turn yellow too.' Most people just ignored me but I got a huge thrill when some crossed to the other side of the road. My new game kept me happily occupied for a day and a half until Dad, informed of my activities, issued a severe reprimand. I was forbidden to continue with this pursuit. Luckily the Department of Education decided that quarantine for family members of someone suffering from hepatitis A was not necessary and we returned to school on the third day.

My game then well and truly backfired on me as none of my friends would let me near them in case I 'really was a leper'.

Word Puzzle

Paul Gannon

T HE FIRST THING JIMMY GAVE ME was a manual alphabet
card. Since he was deaf and blind he could talk to you
only when he held up his left hand as a blank surface for you to
'talk' to him. He was correct when he said that it would only
take about twenty minutes for me to get the hang of it. The five
fingers were the vowels and the consonants were quickly
learned when you joined him in conversation.

The man could talk about anything. Ideas that I had
about people with a sensory impairment were soon smashed.
He was interested in life and thus an interesting man. He
travelled the world as a hobby. He operated a sewing machine
because it was said that someone with a sensory impairment
could not safely use machinery. That was just the sort of
challenge that Jimmy relished. He had worked every machine
in the factory but preferred sewing.

'Would you like to do the crossword?' his question surprised me. I should have expected him to be into a word puzzle. I still had my preconceptions about a man who could neither see nor hear.

'Sure, but we don't have long to knock it over.' Jimmy's face held a knowing smile. Since he had already developed an impressive vocabulary, I asked him why.

'Well' (he spelled out on his left hand) 'I read Braille. When they write Braille, they censor, and abbreviate words. Most of the time that's OK, but it's easy to lose sight of the more subtle aspects of English. When I do crosswords, I have to get right into the essence of words. That makes sure I stay up with the changes that seem to happen all the time with English. People who set crosswords love working in that area.'

His answer will give you some idea of the man I ended up feeding clues to every day at morning tea. As I got better at using the deaf manual alphabet and Jimmy got better at cracking the puzzles, we set ourselves the target of completing the crossword in our morning tea break. I soon learned I couldn't fool him. He would prompt me, 'Did we answer eighteen across?' he would innocently enquire on the blank canvas that was his left hand.

'Oh. No. I missed that one.' I'd give him the clue. I wondered at the image he held in his head that allowed him to never miss one. Never.

One day I was feeding clues at a furious rate (great for my finger spelling skills) and I gave Jimmy the next clue, 'Extermination of a race of people, eight letters.' I was getting ready to ink in the answer when I noticed my silent mate sitting with his hands clenched. This was our sign that he was stumped, a rare occurrence. He sat, his face crumpled in puzzlement. He opened his hands, palms outspread. He did not know the answer. Jimmy actually enjoyed this situation. This was how he learned a new word.

I spelled out the answer. 'G-e-n-o-c i-d-e. What the Nazis did to the Jews in World War Two, Pol Pot in Cambodia.' Jimmy nodded and then sat in reflection - hands clenched as he stored the new word in his internal lexicon. He straightened up. His left hand formed the notice board. His papery right hand, calloused from many years of manual work, flickered across his raised left hand and spelled out:

'Isn't it a pity that we need such a word.'

No Known Treatment

Liz May

THE LONG WHITE CLOUDS stretched and torn into wispy threads seem to split the distant tops, before dipping down towards the river. In the foreground, on the river flats, the regular rows of corn, tall and lush, impose symmetry on the landscape that is mainly dominated by rugged and misshapen granite outcrops and hills. Two fat rabbits bound across the garden beds oblivious to the figure sitting hunched at the kitchen table lost in thought. She looks up occasionally and stares intently into the distance.

'Where did it all begin?' she muses. This morning compulsion, beginning to bear the hallmarks of an addiction.' Every day it's the same routine and she knows that it's becoming increasingly difficult to break the habit. When she was a child her addictions were mere idiosyncrasies shared by most children - not stepping on cracks, or ordering a meat pie and chocolate mallow biscuit from the tuckshop every Monday for lunch. Now, as an adult, these peculiarities seem trivial.

It had begun innocently enough about five years ago, when she received a retirement gift from her friend. The catalyst. It was small and functional, separating into discrete parts, as well as pretty, being adorned with blue flowers. 'For your long mornings,' she remembers Bernadette saying. 'Just for one. To begin your day, slowly.' Each day she would lay the table with Bernadette's present taking pride of place on the marble Lazy Susan; jam, butter and morning paper completing the tableau. She only sipped, at first, not being able to finish it all in one sitting, but throughout the day she would dip back in whenever she had the urge, until she felt satisfied. That was the trouble wasn't it? She wasn't to know how addictive it would become.

'Why don't I have a simple, run-of-the-mill addiction?' she wonders. 'Something like chocolate or coffee, or perhaps alcohol. No. That destroys people's lives. Something glamorous like shopping - just like Isla Fisher in *Confessions of a Shopaholic*. Sex maybe, - no that might ruin my golfing prowess (such as it is). Look what it did to Tiger Woods. Wait-that was the treatment, not the condition. Anyway it's obvious I must be an addictive personality as I am already on the way to being addicted to at least three of the above.'

There is no known treatment for this condition - no AA, not even a fancy medical term. She knows that sometimes it dominates her entire day. Her 'little grey cells' as Hercule Poirot would say. After all she does have every detective book that Agatha Christie has written and is well on her way to acquiring all the DVDs. Not another addiction she hopes! She has tried all sorts of remedies: gone cold turkey, organised her own self help group, but that just made her totally crazy.

Some of her family and friends have recognised her interest and have unknowingly contributed to the addiction, bringing back gifts from all around the world, although she does prefer the homespun variety. Her son even gave her a complete collection!

The crows rap on the glass at the front door, then hop off, content that their morning ritual is complete. Not birds too! She stirs from her reverie. Action is required. She must finish. Today she is going with the Writing Group to Morpeth for the annual Teapot Exhibition. She pours the last dregs of tea from the pretty blue teapot and cup that Bernadette had given her. Then she chuckles to herself. How ironic!

One to go.

Eight down (6)

Vessel for Beethoven's fourth on grass.

They'll love this one at Cryptic Crazies on Wednesday.

Green Jalopy

Liz May

PA WAS A KID MAGNET - a gentle, quiet, small man with twinkling eyes and a great sense of fun. He was the antithesis of the strong, rugged stereotype, but to all of us kids Pa was better than any celluloid hero, braver than Roy Rogers and wiser than Atticus Finch. He was instantly recognisable in his green, open-roofed jalopy, writhing and seething with a multitude of children.

Pa was the grandfather of our neighbours, a family of three boys and two girls who lived opposite us in a small Housing Commission home in North Parramatta. Their tiny house was filled to capacity and included a backyard hen house brimming with chooks and ducks, summarily removed after someone made a complaint to council. The menagerie was completed by the addition of our dog, rejected by my mother for some indeterminate reason, but who found instant acceptance in this tiny three bedroom home vibrating with the noise of children and music.

When Pa visited the siren sounded far and wide, summoning all the neighbourhood kids, who would throng around his mighty steed eagerly anticipating his offer of 'a ride.' We would all pile in, elbowing and jostling each other to secure the prime position - the back seat. Otherwise you were relegated to hanging on tenuously to the running boards, while others had to be satisfied with trotting alongside on the road for a short duration. Down Jeffery Avenue we thundered at ten miles per hour, which seemed to us to be the equivalent of racing down Conrod Straight at Bathurst. A sharp turn at the intersection at the bottom and then we would begin our descent down Ferris Street gathering momentum and excitement as we plummeted towards our goal. Almost at the bottom of the hill, there stood a huge monolith of unknown botanical origins, whose pendulous branches hung heavily arching across the road.

Screams, squeals and raucous laughter filled the air as we drew closer to our target. We shoved, pushed and poked each other as we scrambled to our fullest height in order to grasp our prize - a fist full of leaves or even more cherished, a branch from this beautiful, shady giant. Any remnant of foliage was sufficient to elevate the bearer to heroic status. My dream was to one day be able to grasp a branch, rise high above the car and swing free, Tarzan like, over the entire world!

I wonder how the Helicopter parents of today would view such childhood shenanigans?

Eyrie Mother

Paul Gannon

The healing wounded bird
Stretches her pulsing wings,
Whistling air flutes her feathers.

She stands on her woven empty nest,
Brings hooded gimlet eyes to bear
On the world laid out below.

Thoughts of her young out there
Away on callow trembling wings,
Cause her razor talons flinch and grip.

She drops and flips into the chasm,
Spreads faultless feathered spans,
And sails free above it all.

Pipes a perfect pitch of call
To those that might know it,
Her young and all that care to hear.

She calls them to her,

So when they come or not,

They know that she is there.

Soaring free,

Showing the way ,

High in air above land, above sea.

Gerald

Steve Jacobson

I T WAS AN ODD NAME FOR A HORSE, but he was called that when we got him. The real estate agent who sold us our property in the country obviously thought that, since we were now the owners of a house and a ten-acre paddock, a horse would be just the thing to keep the grass down - his horse. He said he had ridden Gerald and the horse wasn't a bad hack – the agent just didn't have the time nowadays.

And so we handed over $200 and Gerry, as he became known, arrived. He was a gelding, blotchy grey with a large ugly head, a sparse mane and a huge body. Sixteen and a half hands and solid with it, an ex-pacer who had won prizes, we were told. This meant that while he was used to noise, people, harness, farriers and horse-floats, the one drawback was that he had the awkward gait of a pacer. A pacing gait means that the legs on each side move forward together, alternately with the legs on the other side, whereas in a normal canter a horse moves front and back legs on alternate sides at the same time, if you see what I mean. This might seem a bit technical but makes all the difference in the world when you are riding him. He could canter quite well, but suddenly the memory of nights at Harold Park would kick in and he would revert to being a pacer: the change of gait was enough to throw you – literally, if you weren't prepared for it.

He meant no harm. He was quite the gentleman. When he had settled in, our younger daughter, who was about six at the time, decided that since we had said we could not afford a well-bred and suitable pony for her just yet, she would learn to ride on Gerry.

'But he's too big,' we said sensibly. 'Wait a while and we'll find a pony for you.' (Meaning we'd save up and find one going cheap).

But no, she would learn on Gerry. So, full of misgivings but having coped with a stubborn child for six years, we knew that 'getting it out of her system' was the best way to go. We helped her with the bridle and saddle. Of course he was too big for her, even to mount, but with the aid of an upturned milk crate she clambered up. He bore all this attention without complaining and responded slowly to her urging. To be on the safe side, we had a lead rope on him but it soon became obvious that this wasn't necessary. Sera was a strong little thing for six, with no fear and a massive determination to prove she could do anything that other people could do.

Gerry quickly made himself at home and, with good grace, put up with the other members of our menagerie as they arrived: more horses, a donkey, three geese, ducks, chickens, two dogs and three cats. Gerry was the boss, not because he was cranky, far from it, just because of his size. It was too much for anyone to argue with.

When being ridden, he could be stubborn, and he had some other notable habits. We could drive him in a sulky, although he was inclined to spook at bushes on the side of the road, especially as the light was fading. He learned how to open gates which had been carelessly latched and obligingly let all the other horses into my garden. He loved banana skins.

And he put up being taken to Pony Club. The fact that he was about four hands bigger than anyone else's pony didn't worry Sera and certainly didn't worry Gerry. Barrel–racing was a bit tricky because he was so big he couldn't bend his way around the barrels as well as the others, but he served the purpose until we could find a more suitable mount.

He spent a lot of time in the front paddock near the road and one morning he was there as usual when I drove to work, standing close to the fence, looking over into the orchard. When I drove home late that afternoon, he was still in exactly the same spot. I put the car away and went to investigate.

He didn't move as I approached. 'What's the matter, old chap?' I asked. He responded by blowing out through his nostrils but still didn't move away from the fence. I looked down and realised that he couldn't move. The bottom wire of the fence, very close to the ground, was hooked around his shoe and he was stuck. He hadn't panicked or tried to pull away, but had just stood there all day, waiting for his idiot owners to come and rescue him. I fetched wire cutters and freed him. He shook himself, let out an enormous fart, took a couple of paces away and relieved himself with a never-ending stream of piss. He had obviously been saving it up all day.

Patience personified.

We kept Gerry for years until we left the area; with much reluctance we gave him to someone else who wanted a quiet horse for his daughter to ride. We just hope that his new owners appreciate this lovely old horse as much as we did.

Hello Dear!

Dianne Montague

'Hello dear! Is this seat taken?'

'No, it isn't.' Kathy grabbed her bag which immediately fell open and spewed its contents onto the floor.

'Oh, I'm so sorry, didn't mean to cause that. Let me help you.'

Kathy only heard the words, as her head was buried under the seat in front. *Why didn't it work for me? Everyone put their bags on the empty seat beside them to stop someone sitting in it.*

'There's a lipstick and mascara over here, I'll get them. There you go, have you got it all now?'

Kathy took the escapees from the outstretched hand and looked up. She wasn't surprised to see a replica of her grandmother looking down at her. The old lady eased herself into the seat with a sigh. 'That's better, thought I might fall over with all the lurching of the train. Never do know where to sit: you can't be too careful, you know. I always choose a nice young girl like you to spend the time with while I'm travelling. Are you going all the way like me?'

Kathy wished she could say no but yes was the right answer. *How am I ever going to survive five hours with my grandma look-alike? Maybe she wouldn't talk too much.*

'So, what's taking you to Coffs, is it a man? A pretty girl like you, it must be a man.'

'No, no I'm just visiting a friend.' Kathy had no intention of sharing the intimate details of her life with this stranger.

'Are you staying long or is it just a short visit?' The old lady took a breath and then continued on before Kathy had to reply. 'I'm going to visit my son. He's a doctor in Coffs. Getting over a divorce, messy business. She took him for everything. I did warn him about her but he wouldn't listen. Anyway, he's better off without her. You married dear?'

Kathy waited until she knew that no more words were coming out. 'No, I'm not married.'

The old lady leant very close to Kathy and patted her

hand. 'Oh well, you've plenty of time. These days girls have babies when they're in their thirties. Goodness, we couldn't wait when I was a girl. Soon as I turned twenty one I wanted one. Lucky I was married. You couldn't have a baby unless you were married back then. Not like that now-a-days. Anyone will do. Hardly know them and they hop into bed.'

Kathy wanted this to end. Only four and a half hours to go. *Maybe if I read she'll get the message.* Kathy plunged her hand into her bag and presto out came her latest book. It looked so inviting.

'What are you reading dear? Do you do much reading? I love reading but my eyes aren't what they used to be. Have to get those big print books. Forgot it I did. Left it on the bed. Love reading too. Lucky I have you to keep me company otherwise I'd be very bored. Forgot the book but remembered the photos. Robert, my son, wanted to see the old photos. Must be feeling a bit lonely, he must. Do you want to see them? Here they are. Put your book down so you can have them on your lap. Now, this one is me and my late husband, Harold. Died ten years ago. Really miss him I do. We would have been married sixty years this May. And this is one of Robert and Christine when they were just littlies.'

If the old lady had been looking she would have seen the shutters close down on Kathy's eyes. *I don't believe this,* Kathy thought. *How am I ever going to get away from her? I could go to the toilet but I can't stay there for hours. This is like something out of a nightmare, but worse.*

'This is when Robert graduated. Isn't he handsome? You'd like him and he'd like you too. Maybe you could visit when you're in Coffs. He needs a new woman in his life. Then you could have babies. His last wife didn't want children, but I can tell you do.'

'How do you know?' The words burst out of Kathy's mouth. *Oh, no I've done it now,* she thought.

'Oh, I can tell by your eyes. Kind eyes you have. You must be kind to listen to an old lady like me prattle on for hours. You'd be a lovely mum. Good listener.'

Kathy had had enough. 'Really I don't think I want to talk about my private life with you. Not that I want to be rude but I just want to sit quietly and read my book. Is that okay?'

'Of course dear, of course. I understand. I'll go and find somewhere else to sit. You just sit quietly there on your own.'

'No, you don't have to move.' Kathy felt terrible. 'I didn't mean for you to move, I just wanted to read, really.'

'That's okay dear.' She patted Kathy's hand again. 'I know when I'm not wanted.'

The old lady rose regally from the seat and staggered down the aisle before Kathy could stop her. *Oh, well, I guess it's better that she's gone.* Kathy knew that she wouldn't be able to read. She felt so terrible about the old lady. *I didn't even find out her name,* she thought.

The hours dragged by. Kathy did manage to read and luckily no one else came to occupy the seat next to her. She wondered which poor soul the old lady had chosen to sit next to.

At last the train pulled into Coffs Harbour. With her suitcase wheeling behind Kathy walked the platform to the exit. *I hope I'll enjoy this time away,* she thought. *It's strange going on holiday on my own but it's been a year since Darren left and I need to get away. Sad that it ended after so long together but he never wanted children. Maybe I'll meet someone up here, you never know.*

Then she saw the old lady clinging to the arm of a young girl.

'This way, here he is, over here.' The old lady was steering the pretty young girl in the direction of a tall man.

Well, she did find someone after all, Kathy smiled. *Obviously one more tolerant than me.* The man kissed the old lady on the cheek and shook hands with the girl. Kathy didn't recognise the man from the photo of the graduation, but it was obviously the 'Divorced Doctor'. She did however notice how smart he looked and how good looking he was. She also noticed how he took the bags from the old lady and the young girl and put them in the boot of a very expensive car.

Oh no! I've done it now. I've lost a good opportunity to meet someone. Kathy felt deflated. *It's the beginning of the holiday and already a disappointment.* Then a sudden consoling thought came to her.

If I get him I also get the old lady. Kathy walked off with renewed energy.

Blind Date

Steve Jacobson

'Hi, how are you? You seem to have been away for ages – how was your holiday? Me? I'm fine, thanks. I suppose you're dying to know how the blind date went with the Dutchman. Well, thanks for introducing us; I have to say it was a new experience! Yes, I know I was a bit desperate for male company - it's been a long time since the divorce.

'Yes, the first date was fine. We went out for dinner - that new restaurant down by the beach. Quite a pleasant evening. Then we met again - quite a few times, actually. But not any more, it didn't end too well. It's OK, I'm not sorry really. Do you want to know what happened?

'I suppose you know he's the local TV repairman? I didn't know, not having a tele. Not that it matters, but the TV was actually the cause of the trouble.

'We had a couple of dates – went to the cinema one night

– you know, the movie that was on for ages at the Odeon, I forget what it was. We met up for a drink another night but it's been so hard to get babysitters and, after that, it was easier for him to come here.

'Yes, well, maybe it wasn't a good idea, I don't know. I think he was separated or divorced or something, certainly living on his own – I didn't go to his place at all. He didn't talk much about his personal life but he had quite a few interests: skiing being one of them - did a lot of that, apparently. In fact, he asked me to go with him one weekend down to the snow, but I had to say no. Well, a baby-sitter for one thing. Yes, I know you would have had them if you'd been here, but I just didn't get around to finding anyone else. Anyway.....he'd call around after he shut the shop and we'd have a glass of wine together while I cooked dinner for us both. It was nice to have another adult around for a change (no reflection on your company, but you know what I mean). We'd chat over dinner and usually end up in bed after I'd made sure the kids were asleep. Don't worry, I'm not going to go into details. All quite pleasant but not world-shattering – domestic almost, you could say. Yes, I know I've just escaped from all that, but still.

'He talked a lot about his business - seemed to have quite a good opinion of himself but I put that down to his being

Dutch. I know that's not politically correct but I do find the Dutch tend to be rather self-opinionated. He thought most of his customers were idiots but the stories he had to tell were quite amusing, especially his gossip about house-calls to local ladies whose sets needed fixing. But he was intelligent and seemed generally interested in current affairs: he was never lost for something to talk about. So what was the problem?

'Well, to start with, he just liked the sound of his own voice. He wasn't interested in anything I had to say and obviously thought women shouldn't have strong views on anything. Yes, I know I do, that was the trouble. Well, I mean, how can you have a conversation with someone without saying what you personally feel or think? You end up being just a listening post. Whenever I ventured an opinion, he mostly ignored it and carried on talking as if he hadn't heard.

'I suppose he was a misogynist in some ways – you know, one of those men who think that a woman's place is in the kitchen or the bedroom and, since most women can't cook, that only leaves one avenue for approval. Women certainly shouldn't speak their minds, oh no!

'What happened in the end? Well, the crunch came one evening as we were sitting over dinner, he suddenly said:

'When I come next, I'll bring you a television set and install it for you. I've got a couple of spare secondhand ones at the shop.'

'I said: 'I can't afford to buy a TV, that's why we haven't got one. My ex took the television when we split up.'

'I'm giving you one' he replied. 'I'm sure your kids would like it and, anyway, it means I can watch it when I come and visit you!'

'Well, honestly! I'm afraid I took exception to that – wouldn't you have done? Talk about a put-down!

'I said: 'I couldn't take one for nothing.' But of course, it wouldn't have been for nothing; and I didn't delude myself that it would just be in exchange for the few meals I cooked for him.

'We didn't talk about it any more that night. Then I'm afraid I did one of those unforgivable things I do sometimes. You know, saying something peculiar or inappropriate and not knowing quite why I've said it.

'As he about to leave, I said: 'Oh, it's garbage night! Would you mind taking the bin up to the road for me on your way out?'

'I thought he looked a bit surprised but he said "OK, I'll see you later then.'

'But he didn't see me later, in fact I haven't seen or heard from him since. Funny that. I suppose he took offence at being asked to do one of my chores, or maybe it was because I didn't want his blasted secondhand tele. Or maybe I was too opinionated for him. Anyway, whatever it was, it certainly got rid of him!

'I'd better go; the kids are waiting for their bedtime story. What did you say? Do I want another blind date? Yes, I know you know plenty of people, but I think I'll give it a miss, thanks all the same.

Near Gloucester

Margaret Collett

These things will I hoard in my heart,

hold them to me, until my winter comes

then I can take them out, still warm,

and turn them over in my mind.

Cows with backs like bony horizons –

leaden toys placed by a tidy child –

pose for a kitchen calendar.

In the rain, slim gums in army camouflage

form a gleaming honour guard beside the road.

Don't go too close. They will not let you pass;

but stand to keep the secret code

of the bush crouching behind.

Cockatoos shredding the trees and tearing the sky apart.

An eagle lies and floats and drifts on blue.

Grass scraped and combed by the wind.

Hills as round as milk-full breasts.

I would fling myself upon these hills,

until my hair becomes the grass, my body the heaving curve

of hill. And the wind, the wind would be wild in me,

and then be still.

Monsters in the Night

Hilary Kite

Thunderbolts Way -

the road we mark as ours.

The way of bushrangers of times gone by.

Thud of hooves, clink of bridle,

murmur of voices,

thieving and stealthy.

Now

I hear monsters in the night.

Not ghosts of bygone days,

but real monsters intruding on my dreams.

Forcing me from nocturnal fantasies.

The still night air roused by a distant

thunder and rumble.

I wait in anticipation – breath held.

It is coming, coming, coming -

rattling, wheezing, grating.

My fingers stuffed in ears,

head buried in the pillow

of forgotten dreams.

But still the clamour - until gradually,

as if to tease,

it is going, going, going.

The last moan and sigh,

peace.

But no - another, then another.

Arriving, then receding–

marking the ebb and flow of my fitful dozing.

Awake to day's full light,

I try to dispel the memories

of these taunting monsters of the pre-dawn.

But, carnage -

animals slaughtered,

thrown aside - mangled stinking fur.

And that other destruction -

forests raped,

that keep these monsters

coming and going, coming and going.

Thunderbolts Way -

the road we mark as ours.

The way of bushrangers of times gone by

Now thundering wheels -

hiss of compression brakes.

The way of thieves -

of a different sort.

About the Authors

Marg Collett believes being a member of this U3A group has given her an impetus to write regularly. The feedback and support from the other writers has been invaluable to her development.. Her first love is poetry and she enjoys experimenting with prose poetry.

Chris Dean is constantly inspired by the writing group. Her favourite colour is the type of transparent blue that reflects her writings on the river, the sea and a wide sky.

Judy Farley's family has lived in the Gloucester district for over 150 years. After many years working as a registered nurse, she retired and is enjoying writing as a hobby with the U3A group. She prefers to delve into her mind's filing cabinet to write memoirs, but would like to attempt poetry as well. She wishes she had recorded more stories from grandparents no longer able to share them.

Paul Gannon escaped to Gloucester twenty years ago which means he is still considered a 'Johnny Come Lately'. He loves words and how they help us understand each other. Paul writes in any genre that is right for what he wants to say. When he is not trapped in 'the prison of the pen' he renovates his and his partner's hundred year old cottage. These 'labours of love' compete for his attention.

Steve Jacobson never uses her given name of Stephanie – she knows this is confusing, but 'twas ever thus. Born in Sussex, England, she has lived in Australia since 1965. She joined the Group a few years ago, hoping it would help with the discipline required to write a book. It has done that and so much more.

Hilary Kite, originally a South African, has been an Australian for 25 years. She has lived for a time in a number of other countries - Swaziland, Namibia, USA, India and Papua New Guinea. These diverse and rich life experiences have given her the (mostly autobiographical) stories that she shares in this book.

Liz May has spent most of her life in educational institutions until retirement beckoned. So how does a retired English teacher spend her days post retirement? Why reading, writing and doing cryptic crosswords, of course, and in between times there is always gardening and travel. Being involved in the Writing Group has been exciting, threatening and rewarding, but most of all great fun!

Dianne Montague has spent most her life in the city, moving to a country farm 4 years ago. This adventure brought with it the opportunity to write regularly. Previously focusing on memoirs she now enjoys the challenge of writing fiction, assisted by the critical feedback and good humour of the writing group.

 **Lyn Stewart** believes that writing about one's life experiences is quite different to the kind of writing she's has been used to. With a career in nutrition and dietetics she has written reports of various kinds. Lyn's loves lie with plants and Australian history. "Honing my skills in writing short stories, poetry, and non-fiction is quite different from any writing I have done before," she says.

 **Sue Urby** hails originally from Northern England giving her stories a distinctive flavour. Sue has blossomed as a writer of memoirs and poetry and particularly enjoys adding humour to her writing. She recently joined the writing group and is appreciative of their guidance and support.

 **Irene Water's** father taught her to find humour in situations and to express her thoughts and feelings in a diary. Throughout her life as an intensive care nurse she wrote mainly poems. It was not until she had an extraordinary experience in Vanuatu (a story that had to be told) that she seriously put pen to paper. The book is almost complete but she has discovered she loves writing and cannot stop.